Seven Pouches

A Western

By

Joe Cushnan

Published in 2014 by FeedARead.com Publishing – Arts Council funded

Copyright © 2014 Joe Cushnan

The author his moral right under the Copyright, Designs and Patents Act, 1988, to be identified as the author of this work.

All Rights reserved. No part of this publication may be reproduced, copied, stored in a retrieval system, or transmitted, in any form or by any means, without the prior written consent of the copyright holder, nor be otherwise circulated in any form of binding or cover other than that in which it is published and without a similar condition being imposed on the subsequent purchaser.

A CIP catalogue record for this title is available from the British Library.

Commissions, permissions, invitations, etc to joecushnan@aol.com

Joe Cushnan has written several books, most available from major online booksellers, including Amazon Kindle – and directly from the publisher www.feedaread.com - Only Yules & Verses; Rolling In The Aisles; The Chuckle Files; Juggling Jelly; Jack Elam, I Gave You The Best Years Of My Life; Stephen Boyd: From Belfast To Hollywood; Much Calamity & The Redundance Kid; Hamish Sheaney: The Nearly-Man Of Irish Literature; Belfast Backlash; A Belfast Kid; Retail Confidential.

His media work includes: Belfast Book Festival 2013, BBC Radio Ulster "The Gerry Kelly Show", Belfast Telegraph, Irish News, BBC TV NI "Stephen Boyd: The Man Who Never Was", BBC Radio Sheffield "Rony Robinson", BBC Radio Ulster "Saturday Magazine", BBC Radio 4 "You & Yours", The Guardian, Tribune, NZ Management, The Grocer, Retail Week, Edge, Open Eye, Yorkshire Post, The Catholic Herald, Cambridge Evening News, The London Paper, Southern Cross, NZ Freelance, Writer's News, Belfast News Letter, Irelands Own, Fortnight, The Dalhousie Review; Blithe Spirit; The Cannon's Mouth, Poetry Monthly,

Poetic Comment, Bard, Current Accounts, Candelabrum, Decanto, Inclement, Haiku Scotland, Time Haiku, etc.

To book Joe Cushnan for a reading event, a creative ideas workshop, a talk, a literary festival or any tailor-made event to encourage ideas, team activities and morale in schools and business, please get in touch with Authors Abroad - contact Shelley Lee
Email shelley@caboodlebooks.co.uk or Phone +44 (0) 1535 656015
or Joe direct at joecushnan@aol.com

To commission freelance features, book reviews and other media contributions, contact Joe directly at joecushnan@aol.com

Drifter Willard Gammon returns home to find his father dead and his mother grieving. He embarks on a journey of revenge to track the seven men responsible, to deliver his own brand of justice and to retrieve the seven pouches used to divide up his family's gold.

1

The ranch looked quieter than normal. Any time he had visited before, there had always been movement. Horses, chickens and just general lived-in activity. But today nothing to catch the eye. Nothing to catch the ear either. Silence. He carried on riding towards the house, looking left and right for anything, a sign, a threat. Nothing.

He got off his horse slower than usual, looked at the house and then scanned to the left, to the country behind him and to the right. In most worlds, peace and quiet are good things, he thought. In this open country, they were strange.

He tied the reins to a post and walked up the steps to the door. His boots on the boards

broke the silence. He prepared to knock but noticed that the door was opened about an inch. He thought he heard something coming from inside. He drew his gun and used it to ease the door. He thought he heard crying, sobbing. He pushed the door fully
open and saw that the room was a mess, furniture upended and all the domestic inventory had been scattered or broken or both. In one corner he saw his father, sitting, head back and enough red patches to chill the soul. He started towards him but was distracted by his mother in another corner, huddled up and whimpering. He went to her first.

"What happened?" She looked at him and then looked at her husband.

"They killed him right in front of me. Made me look. Seven of them, each one in turn shot him. Said if I didn't look, they'd skin me slow." She was weeping.

"Did they hurt you?"

"Only my heart and soul," she said.

"Did they touch you?'

"No."

"Ma, you would tell me, wouldn't you?"

"They pushed me a little but didn't do anything, well, intimate, if that's what you mean." She looked away.

He went over to his father. He was dead alright. He counted the seven wounds. This was no way for a hard-working man to end his days, he thought, especially this man who broke his back providing for his wife and child. He turned to his mother.

"What were they doing here?"

"Big black beard one said he'd heard we had some gold. Didn't say where he heard it. But he was right. You know your Pa kept it under the floor. Dust and nuggets in a cloth bag. They beat him 'til he told them. They found the bag and then took their turns. A grey hair sat at the supper table, tipped the contents onto the top, used a knife to divide the gold into seven, took out as many small pouches from his ass pocket, filled them and handed one each to the others. Thought his bag looked a shade bigger than the others, but they didn't notice. Gold drunk." She made to stand up. He helped her to a chair. She stared at her husband and shook her head.

"Told him that gold would do us no good

unless we spent it," she said. "Told him, Will, told him a hundred times."

Will Gammon held his mother for a few moments before kissing her on the forehead. "When did all this happen?"

"About sun up. They've been gone about six hours, I reckon. Headed east, I think. I heard the horses."

"I'll bury Pa and then I'll take you to the Andrews place. They'll look after you. I'll go on to town to inform the sheriff and get Doc to come and check you over. And then, I'll go away for a while."

She held his face, looked deep into his eyes and sighed.

"Will, please don't………" Her voice faded. He looked at her and kissed her again. Then he looked at his father. He took a long, deep breath to delay any tears and set to preparing the body for the best burial he could manage.

It took him an hour or so to dig a decent-size hole and about half that time to fill it in again. He stood with his mother in silence, although he was sure she was barely whispering a prayer or something. His Ma and Pa had struggled like just about everybody else to build a homestead and survive. They had loved each other but had gotten to that stage in their long marriage where words became less and glances, instincts and movement took over most of the communication. Will recalled a teacher once saying: "Sometimes words can serve us well and sometimes words can go to hell for all that they do." Seemed even educators got sick of words every once in a while.

Will helped his mother tidy up the house. She packed a few things in a bag while her son assembled the wagon.

It was early evening when they set off to the Andrews place. Will worked out that the seven bastards had about half a day's start. By the time he delivered his mother and sidetracked into town, it would be dark before he set out to track them down. Seven dead men. Seven pouches of gold. That was his job for however long it took.

The Andrews family were as true to the Gospel love-thy-neighbour ideal and took Will's mother in with open arms and loving hearts.

"I gotta go, Ma," said Will.

"I know. I know."

"I gave Mr Andrews some money. He didn't want to take it but I slipped it into his coat pocket."

"Thank you."

"Mrs Andrews gave me a bag of provisions to keep me going for at least a few days."

"She's a kindly one."

"I'll be back soon." Gammon hugged his mother.

"With blood on your hands?"

"I've never lied to you, Ma."

"Then don't tell me."

"I love you, Ma."

"I love you too."

Will Gammon rode out of the Andrews property in half-moonlight. He loved his mother, grieved about his father's passing and felt the devil's wrath as he began his hunt for the men that killed him, widowed his wife and stole his gold.

2

Gammon knew this country well. He had grown up at the ranch but when he turned sixteen he decided to become a drifter, a man for hire to do anything but killing, although he knew how to kill. He liked doing a job for a week or so, a month at the most, and then moving on. He felt free. He felt it right that a man should do whatever he wanted to in life, earn his keep as honestly as possible and stay within the law and the boundaries of common sense.

He calculated the time since the men arrived at the ranch to this moment when he was resting against a tree about twenty miles into his journey east. He knew of a small town, Cave Creek, a couple of miles further and reckoned he would get there by first light. Of course, the killers could have veered off in any direction. They could have split up and be scattered far and wide. But Gammon just wanted to catch up with one of them, any one, and start gouging information out of him about the others. He might get lucky and get them all in one ambush.

Before he left the Andrews place, Gammon's mother had tried to describe the seven men. The black beard man was the biggest, in the tallest, fattest sense. He had a two or three inch scar on the back of his left hand. The grey haired gold divider didn't seem to have a tooth in his head. Around his neck was a leather string with a gold crucifix attached. A third just looked like a sixteen-year-old boy with an ass-fluff, sorry-as-hell moustache. A fourth wore a necktie on a filthy white shirt. He had a Derby hat and a holster with a dragon on it. A fifth looked like a half-breed. A sixth, a scrawny runt, had a habit of licking his lips every few seconds, like he was about to eat something or had just finished eating something. The seventh man was the one that did all the punching and kicking. He had fired the first shot. He was dressed in black, including tight black gloves and had a permanent sneer on his ugly face.

Gammon had scribbled the descriptions on a piece of paper, like a checklist of grocery supplies. He looked ahead to drawing lines through each man's notes as they went on their way to meet their maker. He wasn't a killer by nature or by trade but he knew how to kill.

He took a job one time as a Deputy in a posse that gave chase to a bunch of bank robbers. There was a shoot-out in some open country near Tucson, robbers behind trees, posse behind rocks. It lasted about an afternoon. Gammon had crawled up a slope and along a ridge to get behind at least two of the gang. He called on them to drop their guns. They didn't and he let them have it. In a matter of seconds, they were both lying dead. The others surrendered. He took his pay and refused to let his conscience bleed for the men he killed. They had a choice. Yes, he knew what it felt like to kill.

When night fell, Gammon built a small fire inside a collection of rocks he'd gathered to dull the glow a little. This was rough country and he didn't want to attract the wrong kind of attention of the two or four-legged kind. He felt exhausted, but before he attempted sleep, he looked up at the clear, starry sky and said out loud: "Rest in peace, Pa. I love you Ma." Then he closed his eyes.

Cave Creek wasn't much of a town but it had all the basic facilities – saloon, hotel, stables, blacksmith, a few ramshackle houses and a Sheriff's office. Gammon rode to the stables and got off his horse. A slight man of advanced age was rearranging some tackle inside.

"Morning," said Gammon.

"Morning, son. What can I do for you?"

"Looking for some men. Wondered if they passed this way."

"Oh. A lot of men pass through Cave Creek."

"Seven men. Yesterday."

"Come to think of it, a bunch did ride in. Can't say if it was seven. Could have been. None of them stopped at the stables. I think it was a saloon stop and then they rode on."

"Big man with a black beard among them?"

"That seems right."

"Man in black? Black gloves?"

"Yeah, I saw him. Reminded me of a Preacherman. But something about him told me he was no man of God."

"What about the others?"

"Didn't really take much notice of them."

"Money help your memory."

"No sir. I ain't that kind of man. If I remembered, I would tell you. Why wouldn't I?"

"Sorry. Sometimes I meet people who……"

"Well, I ain't one of them. No, sir."

"Thanks. You've been very helpful."

"You fixin' to tussle with them."

"Adios." Gammon smiled at the stable man and walked over to the saloon.

"I think one of them was a half-breed," called the man.

Gammon stopped and looked back.

"Obliged."

The saloon stank of sweat, piss and stale beer. There were about half a dozen people in the room, none of them matching any hint of Ma Gammon's descriptions. The bartender eyed up his new customer.

"What'll it be?"

"Coffee. A bit early for anything else."

"Coming right up."

"I'm looking for seven men. I think they

spent some time in here yesterday.
Afternoon, evening, night.
Not sure how long."
The bartender put the coffee cup on the bar.
"Yeah, seven did come in. Spent a few hours drinking and talking loud."
"Big man with a black beard among them?"
"He was the loudest. Big laugh. Talked with a growl. Belched and farted loud too. But, if they pay, they can laugh, talk, belch, fart all they want."
"Man in black, wearing black gloves?"
"He was a scary one. Had this look on his face as if he'd just smelled a skunk."
"What about the others?"
"One of them couldn't keep his tongue under control. I don't mean talking, I mean licking his lips like a cat cleaning it's whiskers. He

was funny but I wasn't gonna laugh at him. They looked a mean bunch."

"Anything else?"

"Half-Indian, I guess. He was the quietest. Sat at a table on his own. Seemed to be fondling a bag most of the time."

"A bag. Like a money pouch?"

"I suppose."

"Any idea where they headed when they left?"

"Can't say for sure. From the window, they seemed to ride east out of town. But one went the other way."

"I saw one of them walking into the hotel," came a voice near the stairs. Gammon looked round at the drinker standing at the end of the bar. "Man with a Derby hat."

3

The woman at the reception desk in the hotel was reading a newspaper. Gammon noticed she was good-looking.

"Morning," he said, removing his hat.

"Well, hello stranger. Room?"

"Not sure yet. I'm looking for a man who came here yesterday. Was wearing a Derby hat. Necktie. He might have been wearing a holster with a dragon on it."

The woman thought for a moment.

"Yes, he came in here. Wanted a bath. Someone to wash and freshen his clothes."

"How long did he stay?"

"What's it to you?"

"How long did he stay?"

The woman thought for a moment and

decided this was not going to develop into a friendly discussion.

"He's still here."

"He stayed the night?"

"This is a hotel, Mister, it's allowed."

Gammon blushed for the first time since he was a teenager.

"Sorry. What room?"

"What's your business?"

"What room?"

"Now look………"

"He's one of a gang that killed my father."

"My God."

Gammon grabbed her wrist and mustered as stern a face as an undertaker's.

"What room?"

"Four."

The stairs were covered with threadbare

carpet, helpful to muffle the sound of hard-heeled boots. Halfway up there were no creaks and groans from the timbers. One step from the top gave out a painful creak. Gammon paused. At the top, he walked along and stopped just short of room four. He drew his gun slowly and quietly. He took two more steps then kicked the door in. A figure in the bed jolted upright. It had a pistol in it's hand. Gammon shot three times, certain that at least two hit the torso. The man fell back. Gammon approached him. "Who are you?" The near-dead man's lips hardly moved as he spoke.

"Willard Gammon. You helped kill my father yesterday and scared my mother shitless."

"I, I……."

"Shut up trying to deny it. Where were your friends heading? And don't make me ask twice."

The dying man beckoned Gammon closer. Gammon's ear was about three inches from the man's mouth.

"Fuck you."

"Where were they heading?" Gammon stuck his gun-end into one of the wounds. The man howled.

"I can get you a doctor. But first, tell me where they went."

"Okay. Okay. They're going to Globe."

"What's the one with the black beard called?"

"Turner."

"And the grey-haired one?"

"Vine."

Gammon locked eyes with the man.

"And what's your name?"

"Bleak. Dan Bleak."

Gammon tried to stifle a smile at the name and the man's fate. He holstered his gun and looked away.

"Are you getting me a doctor?"

"Fuck you."

The man started a wheezing laugh and breathed his last breath. Gammon sat on the bed and closed his eyes to regain composure. When he opened them, the hotel receptionist was standing in the doorway.

"I sent for the Sheriff," she said. "Undertaker too."

"I don't blame you. I'll pay for the room damage. I'm sorry about earlier but I've no time to be polite."

"Do you want to talk about it?"

Gammon shook his head.

"Do you want a drink?"

He nodded. He stood up and looked long and hard at the dead man.

"Son of a bitch," he spat. He walked to the dressing table and picked up the Derby hat. Underneath he found a pouch. He loosened the tie and looked inside. Gold. He tightened the tie and put the pouch into his shirt pocket.

"Are you stealing a dead man's belongings?" asked the woman.

"Just taking what ain't his."

Gammon picked up the man's holster and tore the dragon badge off it. A souvenir of sorts. He threw the holster on the floor. As he passed the woman to leave the room, he held up the dragon.

"Now that's stealing," he said, "but it ain't no use to him anymore."

It wasn't long before the Sheriff arrived.

"I'm Sheriff Connor. You are?"

"Willard Gammon."

"Well, Willard Gammon, what's the story behind this mess?"

They moved to some chairs by a window. Gammon related the story from the beginning. The Sheriff smoked a cigar and listened without interrupting.

"I'm sorry to hear about your Pa, son. But that is not a licence for you to become Satan's avenger."

"Well, Sheriff, we won't agree on everything."

"I could lock you up now and call it murder but Mags here said she'd swear it was self-defence. And her word has always been good enough for me."

The hotel door opened and in walked a rather urgent gentleman.

"Ethan Smith, undertaker," said the Sheriff, "meet Willard Gammon who's just steered some business your way. Mags'll show you."

"Very kind, Mr Gammon. Very kind."

The Sheriff turned back to Gammon.

"So, you're on your way to track the other six."

"That's the truth."

"Which way are you aiming?"

"I think they're still going east. So I'll try that way."

"This could be a life's work."

"So be it, Sheriff, so be it."

"I can't condone what you've done or what your planning to do. But I can understand it."

"I'm not looking for approval or reason, Sheriff. My head and gut are telling me what needs to be done. I'll take the consequences if needs be. But I know what needs to be done. And how it needs to be done."

The Sheriff stood up, sniffed a long nostril drag and took a few more puffs of his cigar. "So long, son. Hope never to see you again in Cave Creek."

Before he got on his horse, Gammon leaned the piece of paper with the gang list on the saddle and put a line through the man with the Derby Hat.

"Six," he heard himself say out loud.

He rode east out of Cave Creek, aware that he had had little or no sleep, food or drink in the past day or so. His hunger to catch the killers was greater than anything his body might crave. He was also aware that he kept thinking about Mags, the hotel owner and what his body had not felt for a long, long time.

4

A drifter is no more important in a wide and breathtaking landscape as a ball of tumbling tumbleweed. He – for it is almost always a man – travels according to instinct, at times to satisfy needs but mostly he just drifts as a drifter is prone to do. Sometimes a drifter can drift for hours, days at a time, without seeing anything that walks, crawls or slithers. Every now and then, a drifter comes across some other human soul out for good or evil. It was such a big country that to see anyone or anything was a rare event but today was one of those days.

Gammon had been aware of the figure on the ridge ahead for some time. It was too far away to say what it was. But a drifter develops a cautious streak. He checked his gun. Fully loaded. He checked his rifle. Fully loaded. He took a swig of water and spat out a long streak. At times like this, he wished he'd replaced the broken eyeglass that got busted in a bar fight a month or so back. He rode on.

Distance. Time. Always two things hard to equate. Only experience in open country over many years can help to work the arithmetic. Gammon reckoned he was now about five miles and a couple of hours to getting close to this figure. He was pretty close to assuming it was a man.

Benign or hostile was still a throw of the dice. As a drifter, he tried to avoid trouble but if trouble stood in his way, he would deal with it. At best, the man ahead would tip his hat and pass by. At worst, he would start shooting. Somewhere in-between, he might be a decent rover looking for nothing but a peaceful encounter and corresponding day. Whoever or whatever the figure was, Gammon never lost sight of him. The figure might have been wondering exactly the same about what he was seeing in the distance. Gammon had no intention of changing course or hiding and nor did the rider up ahead. The distance was now a couple of miles. The easy breeze carried little sound from anywhere but it did carry the rifle shots, two echoing cracks breaking the near-silence. Gammon's horse jolted. Gammon steadied him. The figure ahead was on the move, gaining speed and heading Gammon's way. Over the ridge came several other riders whooping and shooting as they chased the stranger. Gammon rode over to a clump of rocks, dismounted, grabbed his rifle and dropped down to take cover.

The lone rider was whipping the reins from side to side to accelerate his horse. Behind him, the three Comanches in pursuit were stirring up clouds of dust. Gammon hated being forced into someone else's business but three on one was not a fair fight.

He took aim at one of the Indians, squinting for accuracy. It wasn't easy hitting a moving man, especially one riding hard. The shimmers of heat distorted distance and increased the odds against precision but Gammon lined up his target and slowly squeezed the trigger. The Comanche in the middle of the three fell backwards off his horse. The horse veered off to the left, leaving the other two to think about what just happened. But if they were stunned at all, they didn't show it. They just kept coming, raising dust like a sandstorm. Gammon waved his rifle to signal his position to the lone rider. His two pursuers were riding harder than ever. Gammon took aim again and shot the one of the left. He stayed mounted but his horse slowed considerably. Gammon took aim again and finished the job. The Comanche fell forward onto his horse's head and then to the ground. Now it was one chasing and one being chased. Fairer. The one being chased reached the rocks, slid off his horse and fell down next to Gammon.

The last Comanche stopped suddenly. He

looked around, saw the two dead bodies in the distance behind him and decided to ride away from certain death.

The man turned onto his back and exhaled for a long time before looking at Gammon.

"Much obliged, Mister," he said.

"Sometimes you gotta help a man."

"Not everybody has an inkling for helping strangers."

"Well, sometimes you see things and you have to get involved or get out of the way," said Gammon. "Those Comanches, they been tailing you?"

"No, not that I was aware. Came out of nowhere. Ambush. Thought I was a goner."

"I thought you were too."

"Name's Ellis."

"Willard Gammon". The two men shook

hands.

"Where were you heading?" asked Gammon.

"Oh, I was just drifting."

"Seems like we're in the same business. Drifting." Gammon was glancing every now and then at the country before them. Comanches liked to see things through, he was thinking. But all was clear, no sign of movement or sun gleam off rifles.

"Just finished some work, " said Ellis, " and got a good payday. Thought I'd ride for a couple of days to think what I'll do with the money. I know I'll blow it but I just want to savour it."

"Sounds good." Gammon was watching to see if the lone Comanche had any intentions of coming back for a last hurrah. There was no sign of him.

"Anyway, it's not spending money yet. I need to cash in this gold." Ellis held up a pouch. Gammon resisted the urge to flinch.

"Unusual to be paid in gold," said Gammon.

"It was the only currency available at the time."

"What kind of work was it?"

"Oh, ranch work, you might say."

Gammon's gut turned over.

"Where was this ranch?"

"Why does that matter," asked Ellis.

"I might try to get some work there myself."

"It was backaways, but I don't think there's much going on there now."

Gammon studied the man's face and noticed that he was young, probably less than twenty years old. He also noticed that under the trail dust on his face, there was an ass-fluff, sorry-as-hell moustache.

5

When he was a kid, Gammon remembered a preacher at Sunday school talking about man's inhumanity to man. He also spoke about an eye for an eye and a tooth for a tooth, not agreeing with those notions but encouraging forgiveness rather than revenge. Preachers were like that. Learning words and phrases and ideas and things to make people feel guilty about, and shouting as loud as they could from their pulpits to frighten people into believing. He talked about the paradise of heaven and the pits of hell. Glory and resting in peace or fire and damnation.

Gammon grew up remembering those sermons but the older he got, the more he tended to believe in himself. Instinct. He was a decent enough boy but not as good a man as he should have been. The trail did that to the human spirit. Some of the things he'd seen and done warped any clear division between right and wrong.

Along the way, he had done a lot of good work, helped people out and felt decent about it. He had also done some things that would make the Lord himself avert his gaze. The death of his father in such a wicked, vicious, cruel, cold-blooded manner was a point of no return. Gammon was intent on revenge. The Derby hat man's killing was a first step. Yes, it was self-defence in a situation he had provoked by kicking in the hotel room door. But Gammon knew he would have shot the man dead anyway, even if it meant in the back.

Now, the young man with the ass-fluff moustache was staked out on the ground beside the rocks. There had been a fight but Gammon knocked him unconscious with a sweet left hook and then cut branches to make stakes, hacked lengths of rope from his lasso and secured him. When he woke up, the kid realised his plight and struggled to break free but it was hopeless. The stakes had been beaten deep into the ground and the ropes were pulled tight.

"What the hell…..?" The kid assessed his situation.

Gammon stood over him.

"What's your full name, kid?"

"Why am I tied up like this?"

"What's your full name?"

"Who are you?"

"What's your full name?"

"You want my gold. That's it." The kid struggled again.

"What's your full name?"

"Cut these ropes now."

Gammon drew his gun and fired a shot into the ground by the kid's right ear.

"Alright. Alright. Ellis Drummond from Kentucky way."

"How old are you?"

"Seventeen. Who are you?"

"Name's Willard Gammon. You and six other men killed my father and stole his gold a day or so back."

The kid's face seemed to drain of colour in an instant.

"So, I'm taking the gold because it isn't yours

to begin with." Gammon held up the pouch and then put it in his pocket.

"Are you going to kill me?" asked the kid.

"Maybe. Already shot and killed your friend Bleak. So I'm in the mood for whatever my head tells me. Big man, black beard. Turner. Tell me about him."

The kid coughed and tried to spit dust from his lips.

"Turner is a mean one. Seen him pick a man up once and crush him to death in a bear hug just because the man bumped into him on the street."

"What happened after you left my father's ranch?"

"We rode to Cave Creek. Had a few drinks. Food. And then six of us left. Bleak chose to go his own way. Guess he didn't get far."

"Then what happened?"

"Can you loosen these ropes?"

Gammon shook his head.

"Keep talking, kid."

"Well, we rode out of town and camped that night about five miles away. Turner said it was time to split up. He said he and Vine would head for the town of Clifton. He didn't much care where the rest of us went but he told us all to be careful and not brag about the gold. Not to wave the pouches around, for a while anyway. Guess, I was a little stupid when I met you."

"There was a lip licker. Tell me about him."

"Got any water?"

Gammon took a canteen from the kid's horse, pulled the stopper and bent down to wet the boy's mouth.

"Now, the lip licker."

"Only know him as Sliva. Kinda fast way of saying saliva, I suppose. He gives me the creeps. I think he said he was going to find some whores in Lordsburg. I think that's what he said. Breed joked that maybe he'd find the Lord in Whoresburg. Sliva slapped him. Breed reached for his blade but Sliva cut him down with all six bullets from his pistol. Even then Breed tried to crawl towards Sliva. Sliva cool as mountain water just took the blade and stuck it into his heart. Breed gushed blood and then lay still. Turner laughed forever at all that commotion."

Gammon stood up and sucked his teeth.

"So the half-breed is dead."

"He couldn't be more dead."

"What happened to his pouch of gold?"

"Turner took it. Divided the contents between us. Mean man but every now and then he'd do something out of character. Sorta kindness, if you know what I mean."

"What happened to the half-breed's body?"

"Buried him back there, about three of four miles that way." He pointed roughy north-east.

"Sliva, for a joke," said Drummond, still wriggling, "put together a cross of branches and screwed it into the ground upside down. He said it wasn't pointing to Jesus in the sky but to Satan in the fires of hell. I couldn't see the joke but everyone laughed for what semed like all night."

"The man in black. What do you know about him?"

The kid squirmed.

"Can't you untie me? I can talk as good sitting up as I can lying here.

"The man in black."

"Called himself Abel. He joined the gang last. Liked fighting. He wasn't too kindly to your Pa. Punching and kicking. But he got answers."

Gammon stamped on the kid's right hand. He yelled like a trapped coyote.

"Each of you shot my father. In what order did it happen?"

"What does it matter?"

"It matters to me." Gammon kicked the kid in the ribs. He yelled again.

"What were you? Number one? Three? Six? Which?"

"I can't remember. Three or four."

Gammon stood up, drew his gun and shot the kid in the right thigh. His howling yell echoed across the plain. Gammon took a step and shot the kid in the left thigh and then holstered his gun. Another yell. Gammon wondered what that Comanche or anyone else for that matter would have made of those noises.

"Just kill me outright, you bastard," sobbed the kid.

Gammon took out his knife and knelt on one knee.

"Now don't quirm and fuss, boy. I just need something from you." And with a swift action, Gammon sliced the left moustache from the kid's lip, taking a little skin and blood in the process. The kid screamed and shook his head violently from side to side, partly in disbelief and partly to deal with the pain. Gammon wrapped the souvenir in a cloth and put it in the same pocket as the dragon badge.

He wiped the knife blade on the boys shirt and walked to his horse. He mounted and looked down at the kid.

"Here's what I reckon. The sun might just burn you to pork crackling. Slow death but you'll have time to think about it and pray to Jesus. Or some hungry wolf might just like the look of you for supper. Or that Comanche might come back with some more Comanches and deal with you their way. They might take your hair but they might just leave you with that other half of ass-fluff growth on your top lip. Or I could just finish you off myself. The last option is that you might find a way to break free. That would disappoint me. But, for reasons best known to God Almighty, I'm going to bet that even if you do break loose, those two busted legs will not carry you too far."

"Please kill me." The boy sounded like his heart was breaking.

"Well, " said Gammon, "if that's what you really want then that's the very last thing I'm willing to give you. So long, you sorry son of a bitch."

As Gammon rode away and even when he was some distance from the kid, he could hear shouts, pleas, begging and cursing until he was so far away that the kid's voice was lost in the growing moans of the wind.

6

That night, Gammon camped in amongst some trees, again attempting to shield the fire glow as much as possible. He ate some more of the provisions that Mrs Andrews had given him and drank two cups of thick coffee. He could have done with a couple of shots of hooch but that would have to wait until the next town and the next saloon.

The night was like most nights in this beautiful and dangerous country, black shapes, blue shimmers, white stars and a yellow moon. He liked being alone but he seldom felt lonely. He liked company on his own terms.

Random thoughts jockeyed in his head about life, death, guilt, innocence, right, wrong and the whole point of existence. He had no time for maudlin thoughts but he did like to think about things that happened, the here and now and what might or will happen in the future. It was like meditating, sometimes like praying but it wasn't as deep as that. He recalled working on a ranch and befriending an old-timer who loved telling stories and yammering on about the rules of life, codes that men especially should live by in the wildernesses that occupied large parts of this country.

Some called it the code of the west but who's to say who has the authority to make rules in such an untamed land. The politicians and big landowners set laws and built fences but most ordinary people had an inkling for freedom and the decency, honesty and truth that goes with it.

Gammon had his hat over his eyes. Otherwise he would just become distracted by the stars. The old-timer was nicknamed Grizzle for reasons that were never explained. He would say that the code of the west is not written in stone and is always subject to changing words and notions. The words might alter but the spirit and common sense of live and let live never shift, unless something truly awful happens to drive a man over the edge.

"Live with humility and show respect", wheezed Grizzle, while roasting a rabbit on a cattle drive once. "The first part is easier than the second. Showing respect is a lot more complicated if you're face to face with a badass intent on crushing your head like a watermelon. But most of the time it's possible to hear the other fella's story and understand where he's come from and where he'd like to head next."

Gammon didn't always look as if he was listening, but he was listening alright. He liked the man's thinking. He liked his sandpaper voice too.

"Keeping your word is important to man, woman and child, even to your dog and God. If your words don't always tie up with your actions, then that's on you and no one else. Family and friends need your loyalty and trust as much as you need theirs. Don't shit on them, ever. And keep your language appropriate too." Grizzle would puff away on a broken pipe as he spoke. His tobacco smell and warm smoke were as welcome as friendship in an ambush.

"Whatever you're hired to do or whatever you set out to do, get it done. Finish the job. Tie those ends up in a tight knot so that not too much of your past can unravel. The past is done. Make it as tidy as you can. The one that pays you is paying you to do something, so when you take the money, make sure you earned it and earned it good."

Gammon could hear his horse getting a little restless. He raised his hat, looked over to where it was tethered, then scanned left to right. Nothing obvious. He put his hat back over his face and his hand on the handle of his gun.

"I'm an old one now, Willard," said Grizzle on an occasion, "and as you can tell, I like talking. I like words. When I was a younger buck, I preferred actions. Wasn't much of a chatterbox. That's what tired old bones do to you. Slow you down with all that physical stuff. But you, young Willard Gammon, you are a man who needs activity. I can tell that. Yes sir, I can tell that. Before I grew into this bent, spent-up body, I stood tall, I was brave, I was firm in my intentions and fair to those that warranted a second thought. I have done many good things in my life and many more that would make a sister of mercy run for the hills. But, I always knew when enough was enough. I was always mindful that everything has a price and not always to do with money. Integrity. That's a pot of gold in my world."

Grizzle passed away about two years ago. That old body of his just gave up. Gammon reckoned that apart from his father, the old coot was the wisest man he ever knew. He carried the old man's words with him as a kind of common sense alternative Bible. Gammon unwrapped the cloth and looked at the kid's top lip. He wondered if the kid was still alive. He also wondered why he didn't just kill him outright. He couldn't answer that question, at least not on this night anyway. Then he ran his thumb over the dragon badge. He felt no remorse. He would try to find where they buried the half-breed in the morning. He patted the two gold pouches in his pocket. He thought of his father and mother. Said some things quietly to himself in their direction and then eased himself into a lying position. He covered himself to the shoulder with his blanket.

The horse had settled down, except for the occasional heavy breathing spurt. There was a bright moon. The night was still, peaceful and quiet. That is until something or someone snapped a branch on the ground about thirty feet away.

7

Gammon sat upright. Then in a clean movement stood up just as a massive shadow lunged at him. But this was no wispy apparition, this was a hard-muscled solid bulk of a man. Gammon was slammed into a tree and a seering pain seemed to travel up and down his spinal cord. He swung his arms hoping his clenched fists would connect with something. The third swing was the lucky one. The big man went reeling backwards as Gammon instantly followed up with a kick to the underpart of his chin. He splayed on the ground for a few moments as Gammon gathered his breath and wits. But soon the big man was back on his feet and pacing towards Gammon. He grabbed Gammon by the throat with a hand as big as a frying pan and began squeezing. With his free hand, the big man tried to grab Gammon's crotch but Gammon managed to raise a hard knee to the man's own balls making him yelp like a beaten hound.

The big man, now doubled up and bent forward, charged like a raging bull but Gammon side-stepped the oncoming threat. The big man's head hit the tree and he fell to the ground like a sack of corn cobs. Gammon walked over to him only to feel his foot grabbed. He was pulled to the ground. The big man rolled on top of him and Gammon felt pinned and helpless. He could also feel a knife blade at his throat.

"Food," spat the big man. "all I want is a little food. That's all."

Gammon could feel the man's warm saliva-spit on his face.

"I can give you some food, if you get the hell off me."

The big man put his face within two inches of Gammon's. His breath was a rancid combination of whiskey, tobacco and rotten meat.

"No tricks or I'll kill you."

The big man rolled off Gammon and stood up with the knife still in his hand. Gammon eased himself onto his knees, kept his head still but let his eyes search for his gun. It was somewhere close by but he couldn't see it.

"I'm getting up now. I'll get you some food from my bag. Not much but you'll have to make it last." Gammon stood up and stretched.

"Who the hell are you and why do you think it necessary to attack a man if all you want is his kindness?"

"Just the food," growled the big man. "Then I'll be out of your way."

Gammon walked to his saddle on the ground and grabbed the bag next to it. As he turned, he spotted his gun nestling in a clump of grass. He didn't like this man. His instincts told him that he wouldn't be happy with a few salt and pepper biscuits and a bite of dried ham.

"Here," said Gammon handing the bag to him. "All I got."

The man grabbed the bag, opened it and started stuffing the food into his mouth. Gammon watched him for a moment before diving for the gun.

The startled man had no chance to react.

"Who are you?" barked Gammon.

The big man stopped chewing, wiped his sleeve over his crumbed lips.

"Just a simple man trying to get through this miserable life any way I can."

"Name?"

"Cole. Just Cole."

"You attack people often? Try to kill them? Steal their food?"

"Way I was brung up. Nobody took care of me. Been a scavenger all my life. Only way I know. Want something I take it. Easy or hard, it don't matter much to me."

Gammon was looking at this bear of a human being and thinking at the same time. What should he do with him? Kill him? Let him go?

"Need that horse too," growled Cole.

"Not gonna happen," said Gammon, cocking his pistol.

"I'm taking that animal, Mister, and if I get killed trying, then so be it."

Gammon had set out to find and kill the seven men that had murdered his father. Some might call that a murdering spree but he didn't want to kill anyone else for the sake of it, unless provoked. This was a situation, he considered, that happens every so often in this wild country, encountering a man with no morals, scavenging his way through life, surviving on taking and never giving in return. What's a reasonably decent man to do?

"You are not getting my horse," said Gammon firmly.

"Well, then you and me have a problem." Cole had finished the morsels of food. He threw the bag away, reached into his pocket and threw something. In a flash, Gammon felt a knife stab his shoulder.

"Thought I was dumb enough to only carry one knife. I'm smart when I want to be, Bucko."

Cole took his chance and rushed at Gammon, but Gammon had clung to his gun. The first shot hit Cole's chest, to the left of his heart region. The second shot caught him in the throat. He fell with a thud. Gammon studied the body for any movement or any flinch. It was no longer breathing.

"Shit," he heard himself say out loud as he pulled the knife from his shoulder. The wound wasn't too deep, so healing would come soon. He took off his shirt and checked, doused water on the cut and stuffed a torn piece of cloth into the crevice to slow the bleeding. He had to deal with it, quicken the healing. Old Grizzle had explained a method to him that was both unsavoury and risky. Gammon stoked up the fire and placed the knife blade in the flame. Grizzle said that the best time to remove the knife from the fire was just before it turned red. The blade was just about at that point. Gammon removed the cloth stopper, refolded it and put it between his teeth. He knew the pain to come would be almost unbearable. He clenched his teeth and raised the knife to the wound. He pressed down and instantly there was the smell of burning flesh and excruciating agony. After about five seconds, he lifted the blade and checked the wound. One more press would seal it. He placed the knife back on the fire and prepared to repeat the treatment. When he was done, he spat out the cloth, doused the wound with more water and put his shirt back on.

He looked at the dead man. This was a drifter's hazard, he thought. What the hell now? If he left him, something would drag him away for a fresh meat feast or in a month or so the snows would cover him or he would rot from natural causes. Gammon had no compunction to bury Cole. Too much sweat and for what? He thought about setting him on fire, but that would have been a beacon to anyone and anything for miles. He decided to leave him where he fell, but reckoned the big man was worth searching.

He had no money, no possessions to speak of. There was a plug of tobacco and another knife, but no gun. Gammon threw the tobacco away, tucked the knife into his belt and then felt something underneath Cole's shirt. He ripped the buttons and heard himself chuckle. An eyeglass.

"Thank you, Lord,' he said looking to the sky. "You sure do work in mysterious ways."

Then he lay down by the tree and fell asleep.

8

As signalled by Dan Bleak before he checked out of his life back at the hotel, Gammon was heading for Globe. But he took a detour to explore some territory north-east suggested by Ellis Drummond. He wanted to find the half-breed's grave or at least have a damn good try at locating it. He wasn't planning to waste too much time but it was part of his mission to see all seven men before he decided to kill them or make them pay in whatever way he chose.

He rode for a couple of hours, his shoulder still aching from the knife wound and his cack-handed medical treatment. When he got to Globe he reckoned on letting a doctor take a look.

Around noon, Gammon rested under the lip of a ridge. After chewing on a stiff piece of ham, he remembered the eyeglass. He took it from his coat, cleaned the lenses at both ends with his thumb and scanned the land before him. At first, it was a scattergun look at specific things in the distance, clumps of trees, rock formations, birds flying, maybe a wolf or coyote way off on top of a hill, general things to amuse himself. But he soon settled down into a slow scan from left to right looking for nothing in particular. On the second, slow sweep back from right to left, he did a double-take before lowering the glass from his eye. He wiped sweat from his forehead, rubbed his thumb on the front lens and had another look. It was quite a distance away but Gammon was certain he could see an upturned cross sticking out of a mound of earth.

As he approached the mound, his horse slowed down. It was nothing to do with control of the reins. Gammon was aware that horses sometimes have instincts about dead things close by. Looking down at the grave, Gammon studied it for a few moments before dismounting. He pulled the makeshift cross out and threw it aside. Using his gloved hands, he started clearing and digging. He reckoned that if this was the half-breed's last resting place, then it would be a shallow pit. And he was right. About a foot down, he scraped away some dust and pebbles and began to see parts of a face. He scraped some more and there was the face of a dead man. It was the half-breed for sure.

Gammon took a knife from his belt and cut a long strand of hair from the corpse's head. Than he stood up, drew his gun and fired all six shots into the dead man's face. He knew there was no point in killing someone that had already been killed but it made a kind of sense to Gammon, even if it was the kind that God himself would struggle to understand.

He walked around for a short time, noticing the scant trace of the gang's camp fire. Then he spotted a discarded pouch clinging to some brush. He pulled it free and looked inside. It was empty, of course, but it was important to him to retrieve it.

Gammon sat in the shade of a tree and took stock of what he had done and considered what he still had to do. Seven men set out on a killing and stealing run. Five men were left. Maybe four if Ellis Drummond had gone to meet his Maker. He still couldn't reason with himself as to why he left Drummond alive. But he did and tangling with the thought and decision was not going to change things. If Drummond was dead, then praise the Lord, thought Gammon. If he managed to break free and hobble for help, his time would come somewhere, somehow.

He thought about his mother and hoped she was coping well with the grief at losing her husband and the worry she had for her son. He would double back maybe in a week or so to the Andrews place to check that she was okay.

Apart from the names pencil-lined on his list, Gammon had also gained two extra knives and an eyeglass from the big man, Cole. He didn't give him any thought beyond that. Finally, before he mounted and got on his way to Globe, he looked at the dragon badge, the scrap of lip-fluff and the length of hair, wrapped them back in a cloth and put the cloth in his saddle bag. He had three of the seven pouches too.

He left the face of the half-breed uncovered. It was all shot to hell and come nightfall scavenging packs of the wild and wicked would feast on the corpse right down to the bones.

9

Globe was much the same as Cave Creek and a hundred other towns, not a lot going on, just enough. Gammon stopped for a while at a bathhouse where he washed, shaved and dabbed some free cologne on his shoulders and chest. He visited a doctor who sniffed at the rough surgery done to the stab wound on his shoulder but declared that while an ugly mess of skin would be there forever, there was no sign of infection.

Later Gammon ate two plates of stew and drank two beers at a hotel dining room. He was aware that he was being observed by a man chewing his way through steak and potatoes and drinking several cups of coffee. The man's star indicated he was a lawman.

In a corner of the room sat the third of the three lone diners. The man had his back to Gammon and was facing the wall.

"Mind if I join you?" asked the lawman.

"No," answered Gammon.

"I'm Sheriff Antonio Brennan," said the lawman, extending his hand. Gammon shook it.

"That's a cocktail of a name," said Gammon.

"Mexican mother and Irish father. Let's just say I grew up in a house of much shouting and plate throwing. It could have been worse. I could have been Pablo Kelly."

Gammon laughed to be polite. Brennan was fat and greasy. His lips glistened from the food he'd just eaten. The underarms of his shirt were damp and the bristles on his chin showed a man not too concerned with personal hygiene.

"Passing through?"

"Yes. Passing through. But I'm on business."

Brennan leaned back in his chair, pursed his lips and squinted at Gammon.

"What kind of business?"

"Personal business."

"All legal and above board, I hope, at least until you get out of this jurisdiction."

"Well, Sheriff, I'd rather not go into that right now."

Brennan motioned forward, put his elbows on the table, then his hand to his mouth before wagging a finger at Gammon.

"No need to get all mysterious or smart with me, son. Something tells me that underneath that sweet scent of cologne there's a bad smell."

"Well, that might be the case."

"Gotta name?"

"Willard Gammon."

"Well, Willard," said Brennan sucking his teeth, "I hope you and I can get along."

"I hope so too, Sheriff. I'm not planning to stay here much beyond today. I'm looking for some people and someone told me they might have come this way a day or so ago."

"Is this a trouble thing?"

"Could be."

Brennan leaned back again and stared into Gammon's eyes. Gammon decided to mention a few things to enlighten the Sheriff and to avoid any unnecessary rancour.

"Some men killed my father without mercy. They scared my mother almost to death. They took some saved gold and spread out across various places and towns. I aim to catch up with each of them and…….well, make them face the consequences of their sins."

Brennan took a deep breath but said nothing in return.

Gammon looked over at the man facing the wall. Then he looked back at Brennan.

"Sheriff, I'm going to walk around town for a leg-stretch. I trust that fits in with your approval."

"If you're no trouble to me, then I'll be no trouble to you."

Gammon got up, put on his hat and threw a couple of coins onto the table. Brennan followed, put on his hat and tidied the belt on his fat belly.

"No charge for me. Sheriff's perks."

The two men left the hotel. Gammon walked along the boards to the left. The Sheriff watched him for a couple of seconds and then headed right towards his office. Inside the dining room, the last diner stood and placed his money on the table. He slipped on his tight black gloves, patted his gun and walked into the street. Gammon stopped at a store and sat on a chair outside. He tipped his hat back and watched the comings and goings around the town. It was early evening and still light, the slowly setting sun causing a warm, comforting golden glow across the roofs of the buildings opposite. He took out his gun with a smooth motion, checked that it was fully loaded and eased it back into the holster. The fact was not lost on him that the man in the dining room had a pair of black gloves next to his plate. Black gloves were not conclusive evidence of the man called Abel, but if he was Abel then he would have heard the conversation with the Sheriff. Gammon wanted to be ready. He put his boot up against a support post just as a shot rang out and caused a spray of wooden splinters to rain on his leg. As he fell to the ground, another bullet hit the chair. Gammon took cover behind a barrel. A third shot struck the barrel front.

He had worked out roughly where the shots had come from. He peered above the barrel but saw nothing, only a street clear of people.

"Willard Gammon? You there?"

The Sheriff was calling from across the street by the newspaper office.

"I'm here. Not you doing the shooting I hope."

"Not me. Can you see anything?"

"I'm pinned down Sheriff but I think I know where he is. Not sure where you are exactly but if my ears are accurate, I think you can cover me while I cross the street to the corner of the saloon."

"Here I go," shouted the Sheriff before firing several shots. Gammon ran from behind the barrel to the saloon wall. On his way, two bullets hit the dust around his feet. He was guessing that his ambusher had backed into the saloon.

"Much obliged, Sheriff."

"Pleasure's all mine. What now?"

"Well," shouted Gammon, "I'd prefer if you turned a blind eye."

"I can't do that, son. Conscience and job rules and all that. But I do have some pressing business at the end of the street that'll take about fifteen minutes."

"I'd better let you get on with that."

Gammon heard footsteps and rustling that he assumed were associated with the Sheriff walking away and laying low for a while. He sidled up to the saloon window but could not see the man with the black gloves. He moved towards the swinging doors and holstered his gun. There was no sign of his man as he peered over the curve of the entrance. He pushed the door and walked in. He was used to sudden silences in saloons. A stranger can almost always quieten a place at least until the regulars take a few moments to assess the situation. About a dozen people watched him and then went about their drinking, talking and gambling.

Gammon approached the bar. The bartender eyed him up.

"What'll it be, Mister?"

"Looking for a man. I think he just came in here. Fellow with black gloves. Might have been a little excitable as he just took a couple of shots at me."

The bartender straightened up and stood tall.

"Mister, I just want you to know that this here mirror behind me is new. It cost me a lot of money after a bar fight a month or so ago. Got it shipped out from San Francisco. Now, I would hate to see it shattered."

"The man." Gammon stared straight into the bartender's eyes.

"A man came in and went out the back way. Can't recall gloves."

Gammon walked towards some velveteen curtains. He drew his gun and slowly eased an opening. Suddenly, something hit him in the stomach and knocked him flying back. The man with the black gloves leapt out from behind the curtains and landed on Gammon. He started punching and gouging before Gammon broke free. This was Abel. This was the man with the permanent sneer on his face. Gammon rushed him and connected three or four solid punches to his face. Abel fell onto a table and bounced back hitting Gammon with two blows to the ribs, then an uppercut to the chin. Gammon fell backwards onto a piano keyboard causing a tuneless clang. Abel was coming at him again with a raised chair. Gammon ducked and dodged as the chair clattered against a wall. He grabbed Abel by the throat with two hands, but Abel kneed Gammon in the groin and ran for the front doors. Gammon was too winded and in pain to react immediately. He hobbled awkwardly and peered outside into the street just as a bullet seared past his ear. He heard a galloping horse and presumed Abel was on it and on the road out of town. He also heard the bartender's mirror shatter as the stray bullet did it's worst.

Gammon straightened up and went outside. As luck would have it, he saw Sheriff Brennan riding slowly up the street. His gun was out pointing at Abel on a horse in front of him.

10

Gammon was frustrated that his plan to track, catch and deal with the seven killers had taken an unwelcome turn. Abel was now in Sheriff Brennan's custody and getting to him was not going to be an easy task.

"What are you planning to do with him, Sheriff?" asked Gammon.

"Well, I'm going to telegraph the county marshalls and a circuit judge to resolve this matter."

"Hmmm. That will take a few days, even a week or more."

"You looking to dish out some swift justice, son?"

Gammon thought carefully before responding.

"He beat my father and then took his turn at

shooting him. I know what I want to do. I know what I should do. But now he's in your jail, I'll have to consider my options."

Brennan took a long sniff of air and breathed out slowly. He put his feet on the desk.

"Are you fixing to bust him out?"

"I'm considering my options."

"Well, as far as I know, you haven't broken the law. Yet. So, I can't stop you doing whatever it is you're going to do. But as soon as you cross the line in any way, I'll be on you like flies on stable manure. So, maybe, to avoid any unpleasantness, you should be on your way. Let justice take it's course. I'd be happy to take your statement about your Pa for the marshall and judge to consider. Or, if you promise me no trouble, I'll let you wait for the authorities to arrive and you can play your part in court."

Gammon thought for a moment.

"Think I'll get on my way, Sheriff. I have other fish to fry. I reckon Abel will get what's coming to him eventually."

"I reckon that's true," said Brennan, "but I trust there's no double meanings in what you just said."

"By the way," asked Gammon, "did he have a pouch of gold amongst his belongings?"

"As a matter of fact, he did. It's in my desk drawer. Locked away."

"It belonged to my father and now it belongs to my mother. Can I have it?" The Sheriff laughed.

"No , sir. It's a matter for the court to decide what he keeps and what he forfeits. I understand your predicament but you must understand that I am taking a lot of what you say and do in good faith. I have no reason to trust you. My instincts are good but not good enough to hand over a man's gold."

"I'll write a short statement that this man was one of seven that killed my father and stole his gold. Good enough?"

"Good enough for now," said Brennan.

When the paperwork had been done, Gammon shook the Sheriff's hand, smiled, tipped his hat and left the office.

He stood by his horse, pulled the slip of note paper from his pocket and drew a question mark beside Abel's entry. This was not over, he thought. This man needed specific attention for his punching and kicking, as well as his shooting. It was just a question of how, where and when.

As he rode out of town, Gammon knew that he'd be back. He would figure out a way to take his revenge of the man with the sneer. But time was ticking away and he still had Turner, Vine and Sliva to find.

He calculated that it would be quicker to get to Lordsburg where Sliva was supposed to have headed. Turner and Vine, according to Ellis Drummond, were aiming for Clifton. There was no guarantee that the men had gone to these towns or if they had there was no guarantee that they were still there. But they were the only leads he had, so Lordsburg would be his next stop.

He was riding the high country when he saw a lone wagon in the valley below. It was not an unusual sight but what caught his interest was that part of the cover looked burned out.

He rode down towards it and was met by a warning shot from the back of the rig. Gammon raised his hand in a peace signal and kept riding. About twenty feet or so from the wagon a voice shouted out to him. "Far enough, Mister. We're in a killing mood right now." The wagon stopped and so did Gammon.

He was surprised to hear a woman's voice. "I'm no threat to you, Ma'am," he responded. "I thought your wagon looked a little troubled. Thought I'd see if you needed any help."

"We've got nothing worth stealing here. Just personal belongings."

"I'm not a thief." There were a few minutes of silence.

"Come ahead, but slow and easy, Mister."

Gammon moved forward, the horse in a gentle trot. As he got closer to the wagon, he could see a young woman holding a rifle. The wagon's driver looked like a child, maybe thirteen or fourteen. Gammon dismounted and took off his hat.

"Name's Willard Gammon."

The woman rested the rifle on her arm.

"I'm Cassie Bale. This is my son Jacob."

"I like to be called Jake," shouted the boy.

"We used to be called Ford….."

"Jacob it is to me and what the history of our other name is doesn't concern anybody," said his mother.

"I'm pleased to meet you both. What are you doing out here all alone? This is not safe country sometimes.""We're on our way to Lordsburg to see my father. He's not in good health and, well, we've nowhere else to go."

"Looks like your wagon needs some attention."

Cassie looked at Jacob and then at Gammon. "We had a skirmish with some men a few miles back. But I shot one in the leg and shot another one's horse. We outran them. Jacob can drive a wagon like a grown man."

"I am a grown man and my name's Jake. Nobody's going to hurt my Mama."

Gammon smiled.

"Good for you. Good for you both. If I might suggest we park the wagon over by those trees. I can see if I can repair the cover and let you rest a while."

"We've no spare money to pay you."

"I'm not looking for anything."

Cassie nodded and Jacob cracked the reins to

get the wagon horse to trot over to the trees. As Gammon figured out a way to patch up the cover, Cassie built a fire and cooked up a simple meal of potatoes, gravy and bread and some coffee.

At dusk, with the wagon in better shape than before, the three sat and ate.

"I'm on my way to Lordsburg too," said Gammon.

"Do you know my Grandpa, Mr Gammon?" asked Jacob.

"Call me Will, and I don't think I know your Grandpa. I've only been to Lordsburg a few times and then only really passing through."

"What do you do?" asked Cassie.

"I go from here to there and back again. I like to think I'm a free spirit. I work when I have to, when money's running out and then

I move on. How come you are out here alone?"

Cassie's head dropped.

"I didn't mean to intrude," said Gammon.

"My Pa died in an accident two weeks ago," said Jacob.

Cassie's head lifted.

"Jacob! That's none of Mr Gammon's concern."

"Well, it's God's truth," said Jacob.

Cassie glared at her son and then looked at Gammon. She was close to tears.

"That's why we're going to Lordsburg. We can start a new life with my father. Can't grieve forever. Can't forget. Don't want to forget. But Jacob needs a chance in life. His father's gone. For reasons that I can't yet understand, I decided to take back my maiden name when I buried my husband. Can't carry the burden of grief through life. If I carry the name, I carry the grief. I don't expect you or anybody to understand that thinking. Anyway, more important than a name, I have to do the work of both parents. Do you know what it's like to lose a parent, Mr Gammon?"

Gammon looked at Jacob. He looked at Cassie. He was close to tears.

11

Gammon stayed with Cassie and Jacob through the night. They seemed to sleep soundly. The wagon horse and his own horse were tethered to a tree and chewed grass. He dozed in between long periods of wide-awake thinking. He was torn between riding on to Lordsburg or backtracking to tie-up the loose-end in Globe. It was a dilemma but he was uneasy about leaving ass-fluff Ellis Drummond alive and now Abel was still breathing, albeit, jail air. He witnessed a glorious sunrise and was content with his decision.

'I'm not going to Lordsburg right now, " he told Cassie as she put their few belongings into the wagon. "I have some business elsewhere. Once that's done, I'll make my way back."

"Well, that's your concern. We thank you for helping us. We'll be on our way. When you get to Lordsburg, I hope we meet again. "

"Yeah, thanks, Mr Gammon. Hope to see you again, " shouted Jacob.

"Will you be okay for the rest of your journey?" asked Gammon.

"We'll be fine. Wagon cover should hold. Appreciate that. I'd like to give you something for your favour but we don't have much."

"That's not necessary. But I could do with a couple of matches in case I need a smoke along the way."

Cassie dug into her pocket, pulled out a box, opened it and handed some matches to

Gammon. She smiled and tugged the reins to alert the horse.

"Maybe next time we meet, you'll call me Will."

Cassie smiled and nodded. Gammon waved them off. He watched them for a few minutes and then turned his horse in the other direction.

He reached Globe by mid-morning, taking care to ride in behind the buildings to avoid being seen. He picked a concealed spot but in a position to see the front of the Sheriff's office. There was no sign of any activity. As he rode into town, he had noticed an empty, weather-beaten barn some distance away from the jail. He tied his horse to a post and headed for the barn, taking care to pause every now and then to dodge passers-by.

He opened the creaky barn door and stepped inside. In a few minutes, he had gathered some pieces of wood and old rags and piled them next to a wall. On a hinge, he checked an old lamp for fuel. It had a drop or two in it, just enough to get a fire going. He sprinkled the oil, threw the can to one side, lit a match and waited until a good flame flickered. Then he walked back the way he came. There was still no sign of movement at the Sheriff's office.

What seemed like an age and a half passed – actually about twenty long minutes – before Gammon heard a shouting man.

"Fire. Fire. The old barn's ablaze."

People started scurrying on the street. Towns like this were wary of fires spreading from one building to the next in no time at all.

"Fire, fire," the man continued to shout. Get to the old barn quick."

Gammon kept watching the sheriff's office and wasn't surprised when the door opened and Antonio Brennan came out. He looked up the street and started running towards the fire. This was his chance.

The Sheriff's door had been left unlocked. Gammon opened it slowly, stepped inside and closed it quietly. He saw Abel in the jail. He was lying down. Gammon walked to the bars, pulled out his gun and rattled it against the metal. Abel shot upright, blinked his eyes several times and mustered the king of sneers when he realised who was standing in front of him.

"Well, well, " said Abel. Gammon sniffed in derision.

"I haven't much time but know before the next two minutes are done, you'll be a dead man. Know this too, I'll be cutting off that sneering nose and keeping it for a trophy, you piece of horseshit."

Abel stepped well away from the bars and started yelling.

"Help. Sheriff, Sheriff, help, help."

Gammon laughed at him, drew his gun and shot him in the chest. Abel wobbled on his feet, steadied himself and glared at Gammon in defiance. He was about to say something when he gasped before falling forward, hitting the floor with his face.

Gammon grabbed the gate key ring from a wall hook, figured out the right key and entered the cell. He checked that Abel was dead before lifting him onto the bed. He turned the corpse's body and looked at the bloodied face. Even in death the sneer was evident.

Gammon pulled his knife and did a rough cut of Abel's nose. He wrapped the bloody remnant in a cloth and put it in his pocket. He turned Abel's face to the wall, covered him with a blanket and stood back to see if there was anything unusual about a man sleeping. He wiped some blood off the floor and walls, stepped outside the cell and locked the gate. He looked again. Sheriff Brennan would be none the wiser, at least for a couple of hours. By then Gammon would be long gone and Brennan would have no evidence that he had ever come back. He tried a key on the ring on the desk drawer. After a couple of stubborn twists, the drawer was free. There on top of wanted posters and next to a couple of corn biscuits was the pouch. Gammon opened it. There was gold inside, a mixture of tiny nuggets and dust. He tied the neck and put the pouch in his pocket before locking the drawer and returning the key ring to the wall hook. He had one final look around before leaving the office.

Back at his horse, Gammon uncovered the nose part and felt a slight grin emerging. He mounted and trotted to the outskirts of town, the opposite end to the barn fire. It was a smoking building now. The citizens had done a good job. Gammon dug his heels into the horse and it gathered speed, kicked up dust and the town of Globe was soon a blur in the haze behind him.

12

Gammon rode for a while, initially intending to head for Lordsburg but after a brief stop at a river to water his horse, he changed his mind. He decided to go back to the Andrews ranch to check on his mother. None of this would make any sense to her but he would uphold his pledge never to lie to her. If she asked, he would answer, but only enough to ease her mind. She wouldn't want to know about the deaths and the souvenirs, and he didn't want her to know. She was well out of all of that.

When he reached the ranch, Mr Andrews was carrying an armful of firewood to the house. Mrs Andrews was tending the front porch dust with a broom. They both stopped when they saw him. Mr Andrews put the wood on a step.

"Hello, Willard," said Mrs Andrews, holding out her arms to greet him. He took her hands, drew her in and kissed her on the top of her head. She had tears in her eyes. He shook Mr Andrews's hand.

"It's kind of you to look after my Ma. I'm forever grateful."

"Will," began Mr Andrews, "we have the damndest of bad news for you. Your Ma, bless her heart and soul, passed away last evening."

Gammon froze. He looked at Mr Andrews, then Mrs Andrews and then to the door of the house.

"What happened?"

"We had supper early for a change. We ate it almost without a word being spoken. Then, while Molly here was clearing away and I was stoking the fire, your Ma sat in the chair. I heard her give out a loud sigh and that was her last breath. I think she died from a broken heart."

"Where is she?"

The Andrews took Gammon into a small bedroom.

"We laid her here. Took a guess that you might be back in a day. If not, we would bury her ourselves. But you came. We'll leave you alone with her."

Gammon stared at his mother's sweet, peaceful face and held her hand for a long time.

He went back to the main room and sat

down. Mrs Andrews poured him a cup of coffee.

"We're so sorry, Willard. First your Pa and now……."

Gammon nodded to acknowledge her sympathy.

"Mr Andrews, I'd like to borrow your buckboard for a couple of days. I want to take my mother back home and bury her next to my father. It just seems right."

"Of course. I can come with you to help you dig if you want, " offered Mr Andrews.

"Thank you, sir, but that won't be necessary. I can take care of it."

"I'd like to get started right away."

"We understand."

"Did my Ma say much while she was here?" asked Gammon.

"Well, she was quiet for most of the time but every now and then she'd recall a memory or two, you know, when they first came to this part of the country. She said that was her dream. Her own place, a husband to take care of her and a baby on the way. But mostly, she stared out the window or at the oil lamp flame. It can't have been easy for her. Every so often she'd start to say "if only" but sat back and said no more. What about you, son? What have you been doing?"

Gammon looked at Mr Andrews.

"Oh, I've been helping God with his justice."

"I don't know what that means but I'll leave it there," said Mr Andrews. "I'll go and get a few things ready."

Mr Andrews prepared the buckboard and brought it round to the front of the ranch house. He checked the horse's harness and put a wide shovel in the back. Mrs Andrews helped Gammon wrap his mother's body in blankets. He carried her out and placed her gently in the back of the rig. As he said his goodbyes, Mrs Andrews gave him a bundle of food provisions.

"That money you left in my coat, we haven't used it. I'll get it for you, " said Mr Andrews.

"No, you keep it. It's a token of how much I appreciate what you've done. Buy something nice for Mrs Andrews."

The journey back home was only a couple of hours but it seemed like a lifetime. As he steered along the final curve to the homestead, it was just like that fateful day. It was quieter than normal. Any time he had visited before his father's murder, there had always been movement. Horses, chickens and just general lived-in activity. But today like that day, nothing to catch the eye. Nothing to catch the ear either. Silence. He carried on towards the house, looking left and right for anything, a sign, a threat. Nothing. Except, smoke from the chimney.

13

Gammon left the buckboard in the shade of a tree.

"I'll be right back, Ma."

He moved slowly, carefully, quietly toward the house. He was weighing options. It could be a weary traveller taking advantage of shelter. It could be opportunist squatters attempting to lay claim to an empty home. It could be someone used the place and moved on, leaving the fire to die away. It could be outlaws. Whoever it was, Gammon knew he could not take a chance. Benign or evil. Choices he always considered. He checked his gun. Loaded. He stopped a few feet from the porch to listen for anything that would help him determine who was in the house.

Nothing.

He moved to the side wall, climbed over the porch rail, steadied himself, took off his hat and looked through the window. He could see the table. Dirty plates, cups and glasses. Remnants of food. He climbed back over the rail and side-stepped his way to the back of the house.

Through the bedroom window, he saw a man sleeping on the bed. He was careful not to make any noise. He rested his back against the wall to think about his next move. He looked through the window again at the sleeping man. Benign or evil. One or the other. Gammon went back to the front of the house. He sat on a step and took off his boots. He walked up the porch steps, opened the door and eased his way in. He drew his gun. Looking around, he guessed that this man had been here for a couple of days. There was the smell of tobacco and a stale odour of the unwashed. Some of the floorboards had been upended. He moved to the bedroom door. It was opened slightly. Using his gun barrel, he opened the door wider. The sleeping man was snoring. Gammon cocked his pistol and the noise woke the man. He fumbled for his gun but it fell on the floor.

"Don't move," shouted Gammon.

"Who the hell are you, comin' into a man's house uninvited?"

"Oh, this is your house," said Gammon.

"Bought and paid for."

"Enough of your bullshit. Get up. Come on, get up."

The man rose slowly and eyed his gun on the floor.

"Don't think about that," warned Gammon. "Now, who are you? And don't give me any lies about this being your home. This is my home. This is the home of that lady in the rig out there. This is the home of the man buried out back. So, name?"

The man said nothing.

"Okay. Let's do this the hard way." Gammon fired a shot into the floor next to the man's feet. He jumped.

"Okay, okay. I just woke up, so I'm a little groggy. Just give me a minute." He sat down on the bed.

Gammon kept watching the man and noticed that he had what seemed to be an uncontrollable habit of licking his lips.

"Your name wouldn't happen to be Sliva, would it?"

Gammon glared.

"How........?"

"Well, I'll be damned," thought Gammon. "You're the one called Sliva, right? And I thought I'd have to waste my time trying to find you."

"How do you know about me? Have we met?"

"No, but you've been here before. I know that. With six other bastards. You all shot and killed my father and scared my mother, broke her heart and killed her too. She called you a scrawny runt. Guess she got that right."

Sliva's eyes widened as he realised who was pointing a gun at him. He eyed his pistol on the floor.

"Kick that gun away," said Gammon.

Sliva stretched out his leg, hesitated, thought better of it and kicked the gun to the other side of the room.

"Why did you come back here?" asked Gammon.

"Thought there might be more gold hidden away. You know what folks are like with hiding precious things."

"Where's the gold you took in the first place? Where's the pouch?"

Sliva licked his lips as if a sizzling, roasted pig had just been set before him.

"Cashed in the gold. I got some of the money in my coat over there. Spent a bit on man's pleasures in Lordsburg."

"Where's the pouch?"

"What the hell do you want that for?"

"Where's the pouch?"

Sliva looked confused.

"Hell, Mister, if you want the bag so badly, it's in the coat too. I keep tobacco in it."

"Get it. And the money."

Sliva walked to his coat, lifted it off a chair and started to fumble in the pockets. Gammon knew he was a slippery fish and reacted instantly as Sliva pulled another gun. Gammon managed a shot to the shoulder and one to the lower leg. Sliva fell back, only managing to shoot once into the ceiling. He lay there, groaning. Gammon walked to the coat, found the money and the pouch. He emptied the tobacco onto the floor, put the money into the bag and put it in his pocket. Then, he turned his attention to Sliva.

"You know I'm going to kill you, don't you?"

"Well, I'm not in a position to make any difference to that? " Clearly, Sliva was in pain.

"Before I do that and because you know what's coming and because you have nothing to trade or live for, tell me where I can find Turner and Vine."

"Why should I? I can take what I know to the grave."

"You'll not be getting any grave. No headstone or cross for the likes of you. Turner and Vine. Still Clifton way?"

Sliva tried to stare out Gammon but the wounded man blinked first.

"They hold up in an empty hardware store when they're not out working,"

"You mean killing and robbing."

"Yeah, yeah, yeah. You know what I'm saying. If they're not there right now, they always come back to the same place in the end to get their shit together before the next time. When supplies and money run out, they get back on the road."

"Well, I can't tell if you're speaking the truth but I'll follow what you say. I'll find them. I'll find them as sure as the sunset." He raised his gun and shot Sliva four more times.

As he buried his mother, Gammon could feel the beads of sweat tickling his forehead and dropping onto his face. They mingled with the tears in his eyes. When the grave was as neat a mound as he could make it, he placed a crucifix on top and a rock on top of that to secure one of his mother's most treasured ornaments. He did the same with the family bible on his father's grave. Then he stood up straight and looked to the sky.

"You will never know what I became and what I have now become since I was sixteen. You will never know the badness in me. You will never know the things I still have to do. But I hope you always knew how much I loved you both and how it tears me apart to be burying you and giving you to nature's course. I know you will rest in peace because your lives have been decent."

As he drove the buckboard away from the house, he felt sorrow like he'd never felt it before. He had said all he wanted to say to his parents. He would never come back this way again. After his parting words at the graves, he went back inside the house and cut out Sliva's tongue. Its lip licking days were done. Then, he lit an oil lamp, tipped it off the table and watched the flames spread across the floor. When he reached the curve in the road, he looked back to see his boyhood home for the last time. No one would abuse the empty house again. For better or worse, he did what he did to ensure that. The house was ablaze, engulfed in fire and smoke.

14

Gammon delivered the buckboard back to Mr Andrews and rode on to Clifton. About ten miles out from the town, he stopped to rest a while. He took his grocery list of killers from his shirt pocket. Dan Bleak. Dead. Half-breed. Dead. Abel. Dead. Sliva. Dead. Ellis Drummond. Left to die. Turner, the black beard and Vine, the grey hair. Still alive, but hopefully unaware of hell's vengeance that was coming to find them. He thought of the line he'd drawn under his family home, the trauma of burying his mother and father, and he wept for them. He berated himself for his selfish decision to leave them at sixteen to follow some adventure in his head. Had he stayed and worked his apprenticeship as a smallholding rancher, things would have been different. He would have been there to help them scrape a decent living but, more importantly, he would have been there to defend them against attacks.

He was feeling remorse but not guilt at his quest to find and kill his father's murderers. His parents had not made him such a black and white observer of life and justice. His experiences of roaming the wild country and encountering the decent and the deadly gave him a survivor's education. He had a good heart in most situations, encouraged by his mother's love and guidance as he grew up. She loved him but, if she had known about his activities in the days before her death, she would have been ashamed of him. But a mother's love can transcend even shame. He could never bring them both back but he would always carry their spirits with him. As he sat looking at the hills in front of him, he pondered the likelihood that Sheriff Antonio Brennan would be wily enough to put all the pieces together and come up with a pretty good hunch that one Willard Gammon had killed Abel. There was a slim chance that his hunch was not strong enough without evidence. And there was no evidence.

There was a better than average chance that Brennan would want an arrest rather than face the embarrassment of an explanation to the townsfolk as to how a prisoner in his locked jail cell managed to meet his maker. There was the missing pouch of gold from the desk drawer, of course. Brennan might have been fat and greasy, but he was nobody's fool. Besides, he had assisted in the capture of Abel and perhaps expected a little respect from Gammon in return for his favour. Whatever happened next, Gammon had to be aware that the law might have already started out to chase him. It was an unwelcome distraction but he had to keep his wits sharp.

He rested for a further five minutes and thought about Cassie Bale. He hoped she and Jacob had made it to Lordsburg without any incident and that the makeshift wagon cover had held. She was a young woman in mourning and it was too soon to assume anything. But he wanted to see her again. He planned to do that after he had taken care of things in Clifton.

It was early afternoon when he rode into the town. After a slow ride up the main street and back again, he got his bearings. He identified the old hardware store where Turner and Vine were supposed to retreat to after their robbing and killing.

Gammon tied his horse to a rail outside the saloon. He went inside and ordered a beer. He sat at a table by a window and looked out at the empty hardware store. In the half hour he was there, no one entered of left the building. He finished his drink and walked over to the store and looked in the window. He saw no one.

"Bit of a shame that store closed down," said a voice behind him. He turned to see an old man, bent by age.

"How long has it been empty?" asked Gammon.

"Oh, it ain't empty. It's got rats." The old man chuckled.

"Oh," said Gammon, passively responding.

"I mean it's got human rats. The vermin that moved in a few months back and took away some of the peace in this old town."

"Human rats, you say?" Gammon continued. "A big man with a black beard? A grey-haired man?"

"You know them fellas, Mister?"

"Sorta. Just the two of them?"

"Well, there a bunch that used to come and go. But the two you mention are the ones that claim to own the store. It used to be a good place for merchandise but the owner, Billy Daggett, ran out of money and off he went with his family to do whatever it is he's doing now. Saw the two rats ride out of town this morning. You can almost feel the town breathe out when they go and its shoulders sink when they come back." The old man seemed to chuckle at the end of every little speech he made.

"They's bad people," he said. "You don't seem like bad people. What's your interest? Them or the store? Are you in the hardware business?"

This time Gammon chuckled.

"No sir. I'm in the vermin clearing business."

15

Gammon checked into a room at the hotel. The man at reception took a long look at him but said nothing beyond the basic "hello, sign here and the room's at the top of the stairs to the left." Gammon concealed his cloth wrapper of killing souvenirs and the pouches he had collected so far. Then he lay on the bed and slept for a few hours.

Later on in the saloon, he met the old man again.

"Shot any rats so far? Still a chuckler.

"Not yet. I'm just thinking about it. Can I buy you a drink?"

"Sure you can. Not many people ask me that these days. Beer. Name's Stubbs."

They talked for a while and Gammon decided

to follow his instincts to trust the man. He could do with some assistance at this stage of his quest.

"How'd you like to earn a few dollars as extra eyes and ears?"

"Well, Mr Gammon, I'd like that a lot."

"Call me Will."

"Okay, Mr Gammon, er, Will."

Stubbs agreed to watch the old store and alert Gammon about any ins and outs. Gammon figured he couldn't be seen watching the place himself. But a town fixture like this bent, old man would just blend into the background, at least he hoped that would be the case.

Gammon spent the rest of the day getting his bearings and understanding the geography of the town. He thought about declaring himself to the law but reckoned that keeping his distance might be a better plan. He didn't want to draw attention to himself unnecessarily. Besides, it was always possible that Sheriff Antonio Brennan had followed his substantial gut and telegraphed neighbouring towns to be on the lookout.

As night fell, Gammon and Stubbs met at the back door of the old store.

"I'm going in to take a look,' said Gammon. "You wait out here. If anyone looks like they're planning on entering the building, make a noise."

"What noise?"

"Any noise, except a clattering noise."

"I can do an owl." Stubbs hooted.

"Not loud enough."

"How about a cat?" Stubbs miaowed.

"No good."

"What about a barking hound?" Stubbs barked.

"Yeah, yeah. That'll do. But once you raise the alarm, you get the hell to a hiding place." Stubbs nodded. Gammon gave the back door window a firm tap and a corner of glass fell away. He reached in, turned a key and unlocked the door. He stepped inside and was hit immediately by the distinctive and repulsive smell of rotting meat. On top of that, stale tobacco odour combined with aged sweat and sour whisky gave the place an atmosphere that would curl a skunk's nose hairs.

He couldn't risk a light, so he waited until his eyes had settled and accustomed themselves to the darkness. On a makeshift bed, he noticed, amongst various items of litter, a pouch. He picked it up and opened it. Empty. He put it in his pocket. He searched around a little longer but there was nothing of consequence to interest him. It was a shit hole. He was turning to make his way out when he heard the floorboards by the back door creak. He drew his gun but hesitated when he saw Stubbs in the frame.

"What the hell? I thought I told you……."

"Sorry Will, " said Stubbs, "but this gun in my back kinda made the decision for me."

Stubbs walked forward a few steps. Behind him, there was a tall, slim man carrying a gun.

"I'm Sheriff Carlin," he said "What's going on here?"

In the Sheriff's office, Carlin sat on his desk

chair and looked at the two new occupants of his jail cell.

"Why'd you break in to that old store?"

"I was looking for some cheap accommodation for the night," replied Gammon.

Carlin sniffed and laughed.

"For someone who checked into the hotel a few hours ago, that's got to be the lie of the day. It pays to have someone be your eyes and ears when you're Sheriff. Ames at the hotel keeps me informed about, let's say, interesting characters."

Stubbs and Gammon looked at each other and smiled.

"I'm looking for the two men that I'm told live there," said Gammon. "I have business to discuss with them."

"Turner and Vine. Not the ideal residents for a town but they haven't been as much trouble as they might have been. So, I keep an eye on them and they come and go without much fuss. I know who and what they are but they've not broken the law here, so not much I can do but tolerate them. What's your business?"

"They killed my father and helped my mother on her way too. I'm looking to face them and deal with it."

"Now that sounds like trouble on the back burner, Mister. I suppose old Stubbs here has been hanging on to you for beers and dimes."

"He's a good man. He's been giving me some insight into the town."

"Why did you break in to the store?"

"To see what kind of an outhouse this outlaw dirt inhabits. Shame they weren't at home." Carlin fell silent for a few moments. Then he spoke.

"Okay, boys. Here's the deal. I'm going to let you go. I know Stubbs here is not a threat to anything nor anyone. I'll give him the benefit of the doubt that he was influenced by a stranger. As for you, Mr Gammon, breaking in to an old building that has been taken over by two of God's unfortunates is not a major crime in my book. But, and I want you to take heed of this but, first thing in the morning, I want you on horseback and kicking up dust right to the edge and beyond my jurisdiction. That's about two miles in any direction. I know what you're aiming to do and I can't allow it. So, the choice is get out of town or stay in that jail. Which'll it be?"

Gammon knew he had little choice. He would be of no use to himself if he remained behind bars. At least free, he could come up with something to settle the score with the last two of the seven. Both men walked free. He bought a couple of drinks for Stubbs and gave him a few dollars.

"If you head south out of town," said the old man, "about two or three miles, you will come to a bend in a river, four trees well-grown beside it and up ahead a mountain with, depending on sun and shadows, what looks like an eagle carved in one of the slopes. You might want to camp there. It's outside Carlin's reach.

"Cos I know, either you're coming back here

or you're going to ask me to get Turner and Vine to come to you."

"My mother always had a saying about people like you. You're not as green as you're cactus looking. If I came back here, things would get too complicated and you might get caught in some crossfire. Here's what I need you to do, but only if you want to do it. You owe me nothing."

"Look, Will. I'm an old man on his way out of life. I could do with some excitement." Gammon smiled. "Okay. When Turner and Vine come back to Clifton, let them know who I am, what I've done, what I aim to do to them and where I'll be. I'm going to tell you the whole story so that you know me and you are in no doubt about the kind of man I've become. I have killed four of seven men, left one to die and have two more to finish what I set out to do."

Stubbs listened in silence and nodded appropriately.

The next morning, Gammon bought some basic supplies of coffee, beans and bacon cuts. As he mounted, he saw Sheriff Carlin leaning against a roof support pole near his office. They tipped hats. Stubbs waved from the other side of the street. Gammon rode away. The next few days would bring this hunger for vengeance to an end, one way of the other.

16

There is something soothing about trickling water, something calming that helps thinking. Gammon had found the bend in the river and sat awhile just to take stock again of the shape his life had taken in a short time. Once he was a drifter, enjoying his freedom to do what he wanted to do, to work when he needed money and to be his own man. The odd incidents of trouble and frustration along the way were part of the random life he had chosen. He always thought of himself as a fair man, on the side of law and common sense most of the time. But all of that had changed. His instinct for revenge and self-appointment to executioner was something he had not imagined. Seeing his father dead and his mother broken was too much to bear. Any notion of forgiveness disappeared from his head. He had become a killer, just like the men he killed and there was nothing he could do about it now. A series of events had been set in motion and, because of Abel's killing, he was now both hunter and hunted. There were two men yet to die for their evil. There'd be a posse on the trail. Time was not on his side. He could sit on this spot by the river for days. He had no idea how long it would take for Turner and Vine to get back to Clifton, then to be tipped off by Stubbs and then for them to make an appearance. So, Gammon's thinking steered him towards Lordsburg for a day or so to reacquaint himself with Cassie and Jacob. He had a feeling that something good might come of it.

He'd return to the bend and wait as long as it took to end all of this.

Lordsburg was a decent size of town. There was money here, success and finery that Gammon hadn't seen in the recent towns he'd visited. As he rode in, he realised that he had no information about Cassie's whereabouts. He didn't even know what her father did. It was only when he saw the sign for Bale's Bank & Property that a clue emerged. He walked into the bank and up to the teller.

"I'd like to speak with Mr Bale."

"May I ask what your business is, sir?" asked the teller.

"I'm know his daughter Cassie and his grandson Jacob."

"Oh, right. I'll let Mr Bale know you are asking to see him."

The teller went away, knocked on a big panel door and stepped into an office. In a few moments, he emerged with a portly man, dapper in a striped suit, starched collar and blue tie. The man came round to the front of the counter.

"I'm Daniel Bale. You want to see me?"

Bale offered his hand and Gammon shook it.

"Yes sir. I'm Will Gammon and I helped Cassie and Jacob when they were in a little trouble on their journey."

"So you're the kindly stranger. Come in to my office. We'll have some coffee."

The office décor was ornate and it seemed to Gammon that no expense had been spared with regard to comfort and style, impressive to those who came to do business.

The two men talked for an hour or so but Gammon was very careful not to say too much about his activities. Bale insisted that he should come to the house for dinner that night, a surprise for Cassie and Jacob, as well as a thank you for his assistance on the trail.

"I'm a little underdressed and in need of a shave and a bath, sir," said Gammon.

"Make use of the house. Stay the night. I might find some clothes for you. A clean shirt anyway."

"Will this be okay with Cassie and Mrs Bale?"

"Cassie will be delighted. She told me all about you and she's a sweet girl. Tragic what happened to Jack, her husband. But, as I always told them, if there was ever a need, not to hesitate in coming home to Lordsburg.

It will give them a new starting point. Good for Jacob, or Jake as he tries to insist. As for Mrs Bale, my dear wife died some years ago. A fever took her from us. I miss her every day. I'm getting old too and my health is not in good shape some days, but I keep working because that's good medicine. The most important reason to keep going is to do whatever I can for my daughter and her son." Gammon saw Bale's eyes beginning to water and he had to hold in his own feelings of loss. "Anyway," sniffed Bale, "I'll tidy some things here in my office. You might want to stable your horse for the night. I can run you back to the hotel in the morning."

Later, they boarded a buggy and headed for the Bale home. The house was less than a mile out of town. Gammon was struck by the whiteness of the paintwork. It was certainly a grand building on two levels, big enough for a large family but too big for one man.

"It's a great looking house, Mr Bale."

"Please, call me Daniel. Yes, I'm not one to hide my success in a modest dwelling. Besides, I always wanted to hand the place to Cassie and her family when God calls me."

Gammon liked this man. He liked his daughter and her son too. The thought crossed his mind again that something good might come from this.

"Now," began Bale, "that's very odd."

"What's that?"

"Well, in the short time they've been here, right about this spot every day, I see young Jacob running from the house to greet me. Look. No Jacob."

Gammon thought for a moment.

"Maybe, he's out back or doing some chore. Perhaps he hasn't heard the buggy."

"No, no, Will. Something's not right."

Gammon told Bale to stop the buggy.

"I'll go on ahead and check things out."

"Be careful now, son. It's probably nothing."

Gammon walked slowly, watching for anything. The tragic day he approached his home ranch came back to him. He hoped he would see the boy or his mother soon as evidence that everything was fine.

He reached the door and opened it. As he stepped inside, something heavy and solid slammed against the back of his head.

17

As Gammon came round, he shook his head to clear the fuzz from his eyes. His skull ached. The blur eased away and he realised his hands were tied behind his back and his legs at the ankles were bound by a rope. Cassie and Jacob were lying on a bed, both tied in much the same way. In addition, they each had a bandana over their mouths. Gammon took moments to assess what was going on. It was obvious they were in a bedroom at the rear. He heard noise coming from the front door.

"Get in here, you old bastard." The voice was a growl. The bedroom door opened and in walked a bedraggled and shaking Daniel Bale. Behind him, gun in hand, was a tall, bearded fat man. Gammon's face gave little away but he knew this was Turner.

"Vine, sit this old coot in the corner and watch him while I tell these people what's going to happen."

Gammon couldn't believe his luck, although being tied up and helpless took the edge of his satisfaction. He reckoned that Turner and Vine were aware of a man intent on finding and killing them but they had no idea Gammon was that man.

"I know the old man is Bale. I found out that this pretty thing is his daughter called Cassie and that this young pup is Jake. We've been watching this place and the bank in Lordsburg on and off for a while. But you? We don't know you."

"I'm Jack Ford. This is my wife and boy. I've

been away looking for work for a few weeks. Came back via Lordsburg. Met up with my father-in-law here and was looking forward to seeing my wife and son again."

Cassie's brow furrowed and Jacob looked surprised.

"So, one big not-so-happy family." Turner let out a laugh.

Gammon glanced at Cassie and Jacob. He winked hoping they would understand it as a request to trust him. Cassie returned a hint of a nod.

Vine was watching Bale. He turned to look at the other captives. He smiled. Gammon remembered his mother describing a grey-haired man who seemed not to have a tooth in his head. She wasn't quite right. He had one front tooth at the top of his mouth. It made this evil man look like a clown. Gammon decided that when the time came and he was standing over Vine's shot-to-death corpse, the lone tooth would join his collection of mementoes.

"Now, this is what's going to happen," said Turner. "When the sun goes down, Mr Bale the banker here and me are taking a trip to Lordsburg. He's going to let us in to his bank. He'll open the safe and put all the money and valuables in a sack and give it to me. Then, we'll come back here and me and my partner will be on our way. I'm thinking a generous hour to get to the bank and do our business and another generous hour to get back here. Two hours from the time we leave. This man will be here to check the time and to keep you people from doing anything foolish. If for any reason I don't come back in the time, you'll all be shot dead."

Bale looked horrified. Cassie and Jacob looked scared. Gammon stayed calm.

"Let the woman and boy go. I'll be your hostage."

Turner walked over to Gammon.

"Shut up," he growled before kicking him in the ribs.

"Gag him."

Gammon fell over and gasped in pain. Vine pulled him upright by the hair and tied a filthy bandana over his mouth. Turner sat down on the floor beside Bale.

"Now, banker man. Do you understand the plan?"

Bale nodded his head up and down.

"You know if you don't do exactly as I say, these people will die. Their blood will be on your hands."

Bale nodded again.

"Please don't hurt them'"

"That's up to you, old man. Now, let's all stay calm until the sun disappears."

It was at least another hour until the sky reddened and the light faded outside. Vine untied Bale. Cassie looked at her father and tried to tell him with her eyes that things would be okay. Jacob tried to say something through his mouth-gag but all that came out was a muffled mumble. Gammon knew he was powerless to do anything to help mother and child at this moment but as soon as Bale and Turner had gone, he reckoned the odds would be more in his favour, with only Vine guarding the house. As two horses rode away, Vine checked his pocket watch. Two hours.

After about twenty minutes, Gammon indicated that he wanted to say something.

"Shut up," shouted Vine. "I'm not to give any of you any cause or room to play a trick."

Gammon tried again, this time kicking over a small table and breaking a flower vase on the stone floor.

Vine shot up and came over to him.

"I told you. I told you," he screamed.

"Mmmmmer, mmmmmer," noised Gammon.

"What the hell are you saying?"

"Mmmmmer, mmmmmer."

"Oh hell. I'm going lower your gag with the barrel of this gun. So no twitching or it might go off."

Vine moved the gun to Gammon's mouth and hooked it to the bandana. He lowered the cloth enough to allow Gammon to speak.

"Now what the hell is it?"

"Water. At least let the woman and the kid have some water. It's been a long day and it's not over yet."

"What do you think I am, a bartender?"

"Just let them have a drink."

Vine gave out a loud tut, replaced the bandana on Gammon's mouth. He left the bedroom for a few moments to fetch some water. It was Gammon's chance to catch a piece of the broken vase with his boot. It was a struggle. One attempt, two, three and then a good connection with the heel of his boot. He managed to slide the piece within hand's reach and straighten his legs just as

Vine came back into the room. Gammon could see a smile in Jacob's eyes.

18

Vine looked at his pocket watch periodically. Gammon had to guess how much time was left. He had managed to get his hand to the fragment of vase and had to act slowly as he tried to saw through the rope around his wrists. He would cut for a few seconds then stop as Vine scanned the room. As soon as his eyes were not on him directly, Gammon continued. It was awkward work. Cassie and Jacob knew what he was trying to do and through more eye contact, it was obvious that Gammon would need some distraction, especially as he reached the last stages of sawing when he needed more vigorous action.
"I'd ask you to turn away, Ma'am. I'm going

to raise that window and take a piss."
Cassie did not react. Jacob's muffled mouth could not disguise a boy's giggle. Gammon got himself ready to cut harder as Vine relieved himself through the open window. By the time Vine had finished, closed the window and wiped his hands on his shirt, Gammon could feel that he was nearly through the rope. He looked at Cassie. He needed one more distraction to free his hands. For whatever reason, her instincts told her that, although not in a loving mother's best interests, she had to use Jacob. With a powerful kick of her bound legs, she pushed her son off the bed. As he thumped on the floor, Vine jolted.

"What the hell?"

Gammon used the moments well and was

relieved that, at last, his hands were free. He kept them behind his back. A nod to Cassie confirmed that her son's fall had worked. Vine lifted a startled Jacob back onto the bed. He looked at his mother and she responded with as sympathetic and apologetic an expression as she could muster.

"Now, whatever that was all about, son, just settle yourself." Vine was agitated.

Gammon closed his eyes and began to moan, louder and louder as the moments ticked away.

"What now?" Vine went over to him.

Gammon continued to moan.

"What are you bellyaching about now?"

Gammon continued to groan. Vine bent down and this time lowered the bandana with his finger. In a flash, Gammon brought his fists forward and connected a right and a left punch that sent Vine reeling back. He was still standing but Gammon rolled quickly into his legs and Vine hit the floor. Gammon wrestled himself on top and started punching Vine until he stopped moving. Then he rolled off and caught his breath. He untied his own legs and freed Cassie and Jacob.

"We haven't much time. I'm untying you so you can feel your blood flowing again. But the ropes will have to go on again when we hear Turner and your father coming back."

"Is he dead?" Jacob was wide-eyed as he looked at Vine.

"Just unconscious. For the moment."

Gammon glanced at Cassie.

"What does that mean?" she asked.

"I haven't time to explain things now, Cassie. Just enough for you to know that this man will not see the sun rise. Nor will his friend, Turner. Help me haul him onto that chair."

Gammon secured Vine with ropes. He took his gun, confirmed that it was loaded and went out of the room to check the view from the front windows.

"This house is in a good position. Plenty of time to see who's approaching from almost any direction, even in the dark. You two should get some water and a bite of food before I tie you up again."

Cassie grabbed some bread and water and shared it with her son.

"Do you want some?"

Gammon took a nub of bread and chewed it as he watched the road. Then he took a swig of water. He turned to Cassie and Jacob. "When Turner and your father come back, things might get ugly. This man Vine here and Turner were two of seven men that killed my father. I've taken care of most of the others and, as luck has dropped my way, these two are the last to deal with."

"Are you going to kill them?" Cassie already knew the answer to the question. Gammon looked at her but didn't answer. Jacob stayed quiet too but there was a look of awe on his face.

"I didn't plan to get you or anyone else involved in my affairs, Cassie, " said Gammon some minutes later. "In a matter of days, I lost my father and my mother. I buried them myself. Before she passed, my mother told me about the seven killers and something inside just sent me down a clear path of vengeance. I don't know where it came from. I always thought I was a fairly peaceful man but maybe in my heart and soul I'm no better than a prairie dog – out for blood."

"I'm sorry to hear about your parents," sighed Cassie, "but……" Gammon interrupted.

"I hear horses," said Gammon. "Back on the bed."

Gammon tied mother and son again. Then he turned the chair so that it looked like Vine was staring out of the window. He cleared the pieces of broken vase from the floor before sitting down. He repositioned his legs in a rope loop and put his hands behind his back, along with a gun.

The horse noises were getting closer.

Gammon winked at the two on the bed.

"Try to stay calm," he said, before covering his mouth with a loose bandana.

Daniel Bale was the first to enter the room. Turner followed. He was carrying a bulging sack.

"These people been any trouble Vine?" he bellowed.

Bale had moved towards Cassie and Jacob.

"Vine, you bastard. You asleep?" Turner pushed Vine's shoulder and saw immediately that he was tied to the arms of the chair.

"What?" he shouted, just as Gammon made his move. In the frenzy, four shots rang out. One hit the floor. One hit the wall above Cassie's head. A third made a ragged hole in the window. The fourth bullet found a home in Gammon's shoulder. As he reeled back,

Gammon was aware that Turner had bolted out of the room. As he regained his composure, he heard a horse building into a fair gallop.

"Shit!" he screamed, before looking at the others in the room, aghast and shaking at what had just happened.

19

Cassie treated and bandaged Gammon's shoulder wound. There wasn't much conversation as everyone quietly assessed things for themselves. Cassie carried a sleepy Jacob to his bed. Daniel Bale stood by the dying fire, entranced by the glowing embers. He was sipping from a glass of brandy. Gammon's head was full of thoughts, regrets and new plans. When Cassie came back into the room, she looked at both men.

"That other one is still tied to the chair. I could hear him stirring," she said.

Gammon stood up but had to steady himself. "I'll deal with him," he said. "I'm sorry about all of this."

Cassie looked drained. Bale kept staring at the fire.

Gammon walked into the back bedroom and over to Vine. He slapped him awake.

"Come on, come on," he badgered impatiently.

Vine opened his eyes and tried to wrench himself from the chair. Gammon pushed him back.

"Where's Turner?" said Vine.

"How the hell should I know? Has he been back yet? When he does he's gonna….."

"He's gonna nothing," spat Gammon. "He was here and now he's gone. With whatever he stole from the bank. Some friend to you."

Vine's eyes betrayed the confusion and fear going on in his head.

"You were both in the habit of going back to that shit hole in Clifton after all your robbing and killing. Reckon that's his next stop before he runs off elsewhere."

"I don't know," said Vine. "He's his own man."

"I was in that store and I found an empty pouch. Would that be yours?"

"A pouch. What pouch? Oh, wait a minute, wait a minute, yeah that was mine. Cashed in some gold we found in an old mine shaft. Yeah, that'd be it."

Gammon slapped Vine's face.

"Liar. That pouch was your share of my father's gold. You and six others shot him to kingdom come. Remember?"

Vine's face was ashen. He realised who was staring at him.

"You're the one that's been after us. I heard about you."

"I'm that final nightmare in your life. I've already killed four. Left the kid Drummond staked out for wolf meat. Got you here. And I'll get Turner before my last breath."

Gammon hesitated. How was he going to get rid of Vine in the Bale house? He couldn't just shoot him and hope no one noticed. He went back to the front room.

"Daniel, I'd like to borrow your buggy. I'm leaving now to take that piece of dirt to the Sheriff in Lordsburg. Then I'll collect my belongings and be on my way."

"You can't go now. Your shoulder," said Cassie.

"It's something I have to do. Daniel?"

"Yes, take the buggy and that man. Leave the

rig by the bank. I'll pick it up tomorrow. I'll report the robbery to the Sheriff myself in the morning. Right now, I belong here with my daughter and Jacob. I want to thank you for taking care of this. But whatever you have done and whatever you are about to do, well, son, that's none of my business."

Gammon checked the buggy and then hauled Vine out of the house. He secured him to the left of the front bench of the rig and climbed onto the right side.

Cassie stood at the door with her father. Neither said anything nor waved as the rig disappeared into the dark curve of the road.

About two miles away from the house, Gammon stopped the buggy.

"Why are you stopping? Lordsburg is still a mile or so away," said Vine.

"You won't be seeing Lordsburg again. " Gammon untied Vine and pushed him off the seat. He hit the ground and yelped in pain. "Don't say anything. Just shut up. This is what's coming to you." Gammon drew his gun and shot six bullets into Vine's curled up body. He stood for a few moments to calm himself by listening to the near-silence of the night air. Then he knelt by the dead body, prised open Vine's mouth with his fingers and used his gun handle to hammer the lone tooth loose. Then with a tug, the tooth was detached from the gum. He cradled the trophy in his gloved hand, looked again at the body and spat on it. He put the tooth in his pocket.

It took nearly half an hour to conceal Vine's corpse under some rocks and brambles, well away from the road. Gammon climbed aboard the buggy and headed for the bend in the river.

He was counting on Turner returning briefly to Clifton and then getting the hell out of there to find a new base. This latest escapade in Lordsburg and the house would escalate as soon as Bale informed the Sheriff. Things would be too hot for Turner anywhere in this vicinity. Things would be just as hot for Gammon once the account of the night's events had spread. But Gammon was prepared for an ugly ending to this saga. He was also counting on old man Stubbs informing Turner about the bend in the river. If Gammon knew anything about the instincts of men like Turner, he was confident that the fat man would not be able to resist a showdown. Of course, he mused, all of this might not happen if Turner had been spooked enough just to ride as long and as far as he could, making it next to impossible for anyone to find him. Gammon parked the buggy and rested against a wheel. As a drifter, he had developed the knack of dozing rather than sleeping. He had his hand on his gun. The trickling water brought him comfort. He thought about Cassie. He knew he was growing fonder and fonder of her, but this night, she understood him a little more and maybe liked him a lot less. He was not husband or father material, he thought. He had been a loving son, a jack-of-most-trades drifter and, lately, a guiltless killer. The past was a bell he couldn't unring. The here and now made sense to him. Tomorrows were unknown and unfenced territory. Besides, he reminded himself, he might not survive the next few hours if Turner came calling all of a sudden.

20

He was half-awake when he became aware of something or someone disturbing the rhythm and flow of the water. He estimated that it was a short time until dawn. As quietly as he could, he crawled to take cover behind the tree next to the buggy. He waited. The something or someone had either paused in the river or was out of it because the noise of the flow had settled back to normal.

"The man called Gammon," bellowed a voice as rough as a drunkard's cough.

Gammon stayed silent and still.

"I know you're here. I know that we've something to settle."

Gammon couldn't see anyone in the dim

light. From the voice, he had a rough idea of the man's distance from him.

"I know who you are and what you are and what you've been doing. I know you killed six and now you want me."

"Show yourself," shouted Gammon. "Let's talk."

A bullet hit the tree. Turner seemed to be a good judge of distance and location too. Gammon returned two shots but had no idea of the exact position of his target.

"One of us will die before the sun comes up," shouted Turner. "I'm aiming to ride on to new pastures. Things around here are too unfriendly right now."

"I aim to ride on too," answered Gammon. "I want to see you dead and I want the pouch of gold you stole from my father."

"You can have the pouch, but there ain't no gold left inside." Turner laughed from his gut, an actual belly laugh.

Gammon rolled from the tree under the buggy. He could see Turner's shape half-hidden behind a small boulder.

"Just so you know, " he yelled, "that old coot in Clifton is as dead as you're gonna be soon. Tried to tell me a story but I beat the truth out of him."

Gammon breathed deeply and allowed himself a moment to mourn Stubbs. A bullet hit the ground near a wheel and Gammon shot back at the shadow-shape. He fired twice. The first bullet hit the rock. The noise was unmistakeable. The second came to an abrupt thud as if it had met a softer destination.

"You shot?" Gammon shouted.

"You'll pay to find out, you bastard."

"I think I got you."

"That don't make any difference to what's gonna happen."

Gammon rolled from under the buggy and fired three more shots at Turner. He heard a yelp. He reloaded his gun and picked his moment to make a run for the rock, shooting as he went. By the time he reached Turner, the big man was lying on the ground, his gun about a foot away from his hand. Gammon kicked the gun away.

"So, you're Turner." Gammon kicked him in the ribs.

Turner squirmed on the ground.

"Where's the pouch?"

"Pouch, pouch, fucking pouch." Gammon

kicked him again. He yelled and took a minute to catch his breath

"It's in my saddlebag. My horse is tied over the river."

Gammon stood over Turner and reloaded his gun. Then he pointed it at Turner's head. The sun was beginning to appear and the big man showed no fear. Gammon's finger pressure on the trigger eased a little as something, a feeling of guilt, remorse, who knows, entered his head. Turner detected hesitation.

"What? Scared to do it?"

"No, I'm not scared. I'm just savouring the moment. I'm not sure what I've gained by killing you bastards but I hope I've rid the world of several more rats. Old Stubbs would be proud of me for that. Why did you kill him?"

"He meant nothing to me. All I wanted was his knowledge and once he gave me that, he was of no value. Boom." Turner struggled to laugh but laugh he did.

"One thing bothers me," said Gammon.

"Only one thing?"

"How did you know about my father's gold?"

Turner tried to sit up but Gammon put a boot on his chest and pushed him back.

"How did you know?"

"Old fella in the next ranch up told us. I said we'd do all kinds of ungodly things to him and his wife if he didn't give us everything they had – money, jewellery, gold, everything. He said they had a few dollars and some precious things belonging to his wife. And that was it. And then he said that the Gammons always had a nest-egg of gold under the floor next ranch along. We took their valuables and warned them that if there was no gold down the road, we'd be back to deal with them."

Gammon was taken aback.

"Which ranch was this?"

Turner could see that Gammon was unsettled.

"Well now, I think I've rattled something in that skin of yours."

"Which ranch?"

"Think it was owned by a man called Andrews. He pointed us in the direction of a stash of gold. Grateful to him."

Gammon looked at the rising sun, regained his composure and shot Turner six times in the head. Then he knelt down, took a knife from his belt and skinned the black beard off his chin. He left Turner where he lay.

Over the river, Gammon found Turner's horse. In the saddlebags, he found the money from the bank robbery, a few personal belongings and an empty pouch. He climbed onto the horse and rode away, in the direction of Lordsburg, stung by the revelation that Mr Andrews, in fear for his and his wife's lives, set in motion events that would lead to the death of his parents. He stopped after a while and threw up on the road. He took a swig of water from Turner's canteen and spat out to clean his mouth. First he would go back to the hotel in Lordsburg to retrieve his things from the hotel. He would leave the robbery money in a package to be delivered by the clerk to

Daniel Bale, along with directions to locate his buggy. Then, he would go back to the Andrews place and confront Mr Andrews. He had no certainty about his actions once he got there.

21

The last time Gammon visited the Andrews place was supposed to be the last time. Turner's story that Mr Andrews had directed the gang to his parents shocked him to the core. After a brief stop in Lordsburg to collect his belongings and to return the bank money, he rode hard to tie up a loose end. At the sound of his horse, Mrs Andrews appeared on the porch. He could see her shading her eyes and trying to identify the rider. She was joined by Mr Andrews. Gammon dismounted and tied his horse reins to a post.

"Willard," said Mrs Andrews, "what are you doing back here? Oh, listen to me not minding my manners. Come in, come in."

Mr Andrews stretched his hand to shake Gammon's. Gammon ignored him.

"Will?" he said. "Something wrong?"

Gammon walked passed him, kissed Mrs Andrews on the cheek and went inside.

"Mr Andrews, I'll come straight to the point. You sent those killers to find my father's gold. You triggered this whole thing."

Gammon gritted his teeth and stared at the man in front of him who was now shaking visibly.

"I didn't know what else to do, son. They would have killed both of us. I had to act quickly. It was the first thing I thought of. I'm not proud of it and I've regretted it every second since then."

Gammon stepped forward and raised his fist, but he stopped short of hitting Mr Andrews.

"We were frightened, Willard," said Mrs Andrews. "We meant no harm. You know we wouldn't mean any harm."

"You knew when you saw me. You knew, but you didn't tell me."

Mr Andrews sat in an armchair, his head bent. Mrs Andrews stepped forward and touched Gammon's arm. Then she hugged him. It brought back memories of his own mother's love, and he knew he was crying. Gammon looked at her and smiled. Mr Andrews raised his head.

"I'm sorry, Will. I truly am."

Gammon nodded in his direction.

"I came here will evil intentions, sir. I've done a lot of bad things in recent times to satisfy my own brand of justice. I've killed in the name of revenge. One more killing wouldn't have made any difference.

But I know what you did and why you did it. Fear is a terrible thing. So it might take me a while to find that place in my heart that forgives, but I know you are good folks with good hearts. So, that's an end to it."

"I'll make some coffee and something to eat," said Mrs Andrews, wiping a tear of her own. "I suspect the boy will be ready for something too."

 "I'm not such a boy these days, Mrs Andrews."

"Oh, I didn't mean you, Willard. I meant the boy we're looking after. He's in the bedroom asleep. We found him struggling on the road when we went to town. Someone had done some terrible things to him."

While Mrs Andrews was preparing, Gammon

edged his way to the bedroom door. He opened it and looked inside. The first thing he saw was a gun pointing straight at him. Then he saw Ellis Drummond and the remains of his ass-fluff top lip.

"Step inside," said Drummond. "Now, isn't this something?"

Drummond was in bed. Gammon knew his legs were busted and he wasn't surprised at his sunburned face.

Mrs Andrews breezed into the room and stopped suddenly when she saw the gun.

"Ellis, what is going on?"

"Now, Mrs Andrews," shouted Drummond, "this is none of your affair."

Mr Andrews walked in.

"What the....?"

Drummond wagged the gun at Gammon.

"This is the devil rider that shot and shackled me and left me for dead."

The Andrews looked at Gammon.

"I'm surprised you didn't recognise this kid as one of the gang that threatened you. But I suppose his scorched face and disfigurement is to blame for that."

"Shut up," shouted Drummond. "And drop that gun belt."

Gammon unbuckled his belt slowly and just before it dropped to the floor, he drew his pistol and shot the gun out of Drummond's hand. The Andrews hugged each other tightly. Gammon could see that Drummond was desperate to do something but was physically incapable. His tense face showed a man both furious and deflated.

"Will," said Mr Andrews, "I don't know what

you intend to do to this boy but I'd ask you not to do it in this house."

"Mr Andrews, I'll not hide my intentions. I'm going to kill Ellis but out of respect for you, I will drag him outside and dispose of him as far as I can drag him. He'll be no concern of yours and you will never see me again. I have mixed feelings about you, sir, but Mrs Andrews, I will always hold you in my heart as a kindly woman. I know I'm not being fair to your husband in this but that's the way I feel right now."

The Andrews said nothing.

"Now, I'd like you both to take a walk to the tree out yonder and let me do what I'm about to do. By the time you get there and back, we'll be gone."

The Andrews walked out of the room slowly.

When Gammon heard the front door close, he walked to Drummond and hit him hard on the head with his gun handle. Then he carried him outside and laid him on the ground behind his horse. He trussed the boy's feet with a rope, and then tied the other end to his saddle. He mounted. Some distance away, he could see the Andrews in a slow walk. He dug his spurs into the sides of his horse and began to drag Ellis Drummond along the ground. As he gathered speed, the boy skittered and bounced along behind. Gammon had no idea if he was still unconscious. It didn't matter much.

After a mile or so, he stopped. He dismounted and studied Drummond. He reckoned he was dead. His exposed skin parts were raw as butcher's meat. He shot six bullets into the boy's face before untying the rope from his saddle. He left him where he lay.

22

Gammon sat on a high hill slope. Laid out before him was a collection of things he'd gathered in his quest to track and kill the seven murderers.

Dan Bleak's dragon badge and a pouch of gold.

Ellis Drummond's lip and a pouch of gold.

The half-breed's hair strands and an empty pouch.

Abel's bloodied nose and a pouch of gold.

Sliva's tongue and a pouch of money.

Vine's lone tooth and an empty pouch.

Turners ragged beard and an empty pouch.

Seven souvenirs to remind him of what he had done, evidence of the finality of seven executions.

And seven pouches.

He wrapped all of it in a cloth rag – the items, money, gold and his lined-through grocery list – inserted a fist-size rock and tied the bundle tight. Then he stood up and hurled it all as far as he could. He tracked it, then lost sight of it as it fell into a stretch of bracken. "Good luck to whoever finds it," he said out loud.

He turned to face the other direction, took the eyeglass from his coat and looked down on the Bale house. He assumed Daniel Bale was in Lordsburg. After a few minutes, Cassie appeared on the porch. She was shaking dust from a rug. He watched as she beat it against a post. She looked pretty, even in the dusty distance. From the side of the house, Jacob emerged with blocks of wood. Mother and son said things to each other. It was a homely scene. Gammon wondered as he watched how great the odds were against him ever settling down with a wife and child, or children. He had reached a point in his life, either a point from which he could start a new life or a point of no return to normality. But his instincts were weighing in favour of riding down to Cassie and Jacob and taking things from there. He would either be welcome or unwelcome. A voice in his head nagged away saying that such a surprise return would be pointless. He had no claim to any thought of a future with this family. The voice told him to ride away and forget any such fanciful notions. He sat for a while longer, occasionally observing through the eyeglass, but mostly thinking. In a swift movement, he stood up, mind settled, decision made. He mounted and positioned the horse.

The shot came out of the blue. The bullet grazed his temple and he fell backwards to the ground. He was semi-conscious, confused and hurting. He opened his eyes to see blur, nothing clear or defined. He heard hooves advancing up the side of the hill, the side where he threw the souvenirs bundle. He tried to drag himself to somewhere, anywhere for cover but there was nothing much to hide behind. The hooves were getting closer. The blur was easing. He could make out a shape, a man on top of a horse. He felt helpless. He blinked rapidly three or four times. And then he saw Sheriff Antonio Brennan, rifle in hand, drawing near.

Gammon managed to draw his pistol. A single shot echoed across the landscape.

Jack Elam, I Gave You The Best Years Of My Life

Poems & Reflections On How The West Won Me

Joe Cushnan

Published in 2013 by FeedARead.com Publishing – Arts Council funded

Copyright © 2013 Joe Cushnan

The author asserts his moral right under the Copyright, Designs and Patents Act, 1988, to be identified as the author of this work.

All Rights reserved. No part of this publication may be reproduced, copied, stored in a retrieval system, or transmitted, in any form or by any means, without the prior written consent of the copyright holder, nor be otherwise circulated in any form of binding or cover other than that in which it is published and without a similar condition being imposed on the subsequent purchaser.

A CIP catalogue record for this title is available from the British Library.

Joe Cushnan has written several books, all available from major online booksellers – Stephen Boyd: From Belfast To Hollywood; Much Calamity & The Redundance Kid; Hamish Sheaney: The Nearly-Man Of Irish Literature; Belfast Backlash; A Belfast Kid; Retail Confidential.

His work has appeared in the following media outlets: Belfast Telegraph, Irish News, BBC TV NI "Stephen Boyd: The Man Who Never Was", BBC Radio Sheffield "Rony Robinson", BBC Radio Ulster "Saturday Magazine", BBC Radio 4 "You & Yours", The Guardian, Tribune, NZ Management, The Grocer, Retail Week, Edge, Open Eye, Yorkshire Post, The Catholic Herald, Cambridge Evening News, The London Paper, Southern Cross, NZ Freelance, Writer's News, Belfast News Letter, Irelands Own, Fortnight, The Dalhousie Review; Blithe Spirit; The Cannon's Mouth, Poetry Monthly, Poetic Comment, Bard, Current Accounts, Candelabrum, Decanto, Inclement, Haiku Scotland, Time Haiku, etc.

He can be contacted at joecushnan@aol.com to arrange freelance writing commissions – books, features, reviews, etc - and to receive your comments.

For all the young kids playing cowboys in the garden of 170 back in those thrilling days of yesteryear – and we did all our own stunts!

"What makes a man to wander?
What makes a man to roam?
What makes a man leave bed and board
And turn his back on home?
Ride away, ride away, ride away."
    By Stan Jones – featured in The Searchers

CODE OF THE WEST

The code of the West is not written in stone and is always subject to changing words and notions. From various sources, these are the common principles for being a good Western citizen:

- *Live with humility and show respect*
- *Keep your word*
- *Do what you have to do and finish the job*
- *Be firm but fair*
- *Be loyal to your family and friends*
- *Be loyal to whoever pays you*
- *Believe in actions more than words*
- *Be mindful that not everything has a price*
- *Know when enough is enough*
- *Stand tall, be brave but watch your language*

The mean, macho code dictates – look after your gun, your horse and your woman, in that order....and don't shoot the messenger!

THE SEVEN PLOTS OF WESTERNS

The prolific writer Frank Gruber, scribe of many detective and cowboy tales, concluded that there were seven basic plots for westerns. He had a 30-year career writing films and television scripts, including Tales of Wells Fargo. His seven categories are based on these general themes:

Cavalry and Indians story, about conflict, taming the wilderness, identity, survival and, hopefully, getting along.

Railroad, wagon train and Pony Express story, about development of transport, travel and communication, and the challenges therein.

Ranchers, homesteaders and squatters story, about property rights, staking claims and power.

Empire story, about ownership of substantial amounts of land, oil, cattle and anything else that pitches the powerful moguls against the little guys.

Lawman story, about authority figures maintaining order and peace, and catching villains.

Revenge story, about a bad incident that results in a chase and, more often than not, a showdown.

Outlaw story, about the ever-present danger of bandits and other badasses that made the West wild.

The themes are loose and can be adapted, developed and combined for any storyline.

THE EXOTIC PLACE NAMES OF THE WEST

There were so many exciting aspects to westerns for me, especially when I was a young boy growing up in Belfast, thousands of miles away from the wild frontier. Apart from the actors and their characters, the names of the places sounded so exotic and exciting, lands far, far away where all of this wonderful entertainment was set and where all these seductive stories happened.

The States:
Oregon, Idaho, Nevada, Utah, Arizona, Wyoming, Montana, Colorado, Kansas, Oklahoma, Texas, and on and on.
The towns:
Dodge City, Tombstone, Deadwood, El Paso, Abilene, Tucson and hundreds of made-up names for the many one-horse towns of the Old West

INTRODUCTION

This is a book about nostalgia, about a passion, about celebration and, as far as I can muster the skills, about poetry. It's a kind of scrapbook and memory jogger. There will be lists to illustrate some points and poems to ponder as we mosey on through. Some of the poems are simple, straightforward pieces and some are little scenes from imaginary films or just random cowboy thoughts. The book, as you may have gathered by now, has a central theme – westerns – and a particular name and face as it's mascot, Jack Elam, the best supporting actor any western film could have wished for.

This is not a western encyclopedia, nor a text book, nor a biography, nor anything other than a fan's indulgence via poetry. But it might just stir up some fond memories and raise a smile from my generation of pretend cowboys, and I hope it also acts as a signpost for younger generations to visit some of the television and cinema features mentioned herein.

As a youngster, I warmed at the sight of the biggest

stars on screen – John Wayne, James Stewart et al - but I positively beamed whenever Jack Elam made an appearance. In these pages, I'll attempt to explain why as I pay homage to him and the many others whose names featured above and particularly below film and TV episode titles.

I love westerns. I have always loved westerns. I have given westerns a significant chunk of my time and attention through five decades. I stand, metaphorical guns pointing and say, westerns, I gave you the best years of my life.

My earliest memory of watching a western on television was in the late 1950s. It was The Range Rider starring Jock Mahoney and it was in black and white. I remember seeing it for the first time one Saturday afternoon in my Aunt Sally's on the New Lodge Road, Belfast – (always a treat because she gave us a big bowl of hot peas and vinegar, bread and butter and a huge blue-striped mug of tea).

Immediately after the horse racing, or it might have been the wrestling, it was The Range Rider and his trusty sidekick, Dick West. The Range Rider was made from 1951 to 1953, nearly 80 episodes in all. I was a 1954 baby, so obviously I caught the repeats a few years later.

The opening, to the song Home on the Range, featured the introduction:

"...and who could be more at home on the range than the Range Rider, with his thrilling adventures of the great outdoors, his exciting experiences rivalling those of Davy Crockett, Daniel Boone, Buffalo Bill and other pioneers of this wonderful country of ours....and Dick West, all-American boy."

As the narrator spoke, I watched the Range Rider climb onto his horse and gallop after a stagecoach, then Dick West, on his horse, not far behind. It was thrilling to this six-year-old, and on a very recent viewing of the opening to the show, this nearing 60-year-old man still feels a tingle about this and many more western shows and movies.

I watched every second of the action and was so engrossed that the first time I saw a horse galloping towards the camera, I leapt up and hid behind a chair. I thought the horse was going to jump out of the set. It was that real to me.

Now, more than fifty years later, Aunt Sally has passed away, the house on the New Lodge Road is gone and hot peas have never tasted as good as they did back then. But my love affair with cowboy series and films has grown into a passion, and my adoration of the big stars and supporting actors has not diminished one jot. As I both write this and wallow in glorious memories of the hours I sat glued to the TV, I am reminded of those wonderful shows, the heroes, villains, thrilling action sequences and stirring theme tunes from the days known as yesteryear.

ON TELEVISION

On the small screen, I enjoyed the aforementioned Jock Mahoney and Dick Jones (The Range Rider); Duncan Renaldo (The Cisco Kid); Roy Rogers (The Roy Rogers Show); Clayton Moore and Jay Silverheels (The Lone Ranger and Tonto); William Bendix and Doug McClure (Overland Trail); Dale Robertson (Tales of Wells Fargo); Gene Barry (Bat Masterson); Henry Fonda (The Deputy); James Garner and Jack Kelly (Maverick); James Arness, Dennis Weaver and Burt Reynolds (Gunsmoke); Steve McQueen (Wanted: Dead or Alive); Alan Hale Jr (Casey Jones); Will Hutchins (Tenderfoot/Sugarfoot); Chuck Connors (The Rifleman); Ty Hardin (Bronco); Clint Walker (Cheyenne); Richard Boone (Have Gun Will Travel); Eric Fleming and Clint Eastwood (Rawhide); John Smith and Robert Fuller (Laramie); Larry Ward, Chad Everett and Jack Elam (The Dakotas); Lorne Greene, Michael Landon, Dan Blocker and Pernell Roberts

(Bonanza); Ward Bond, Robert Horton, Frank McGrath (Wagon Train); Fess Parker (Daniel Boone); Richard Long, Lee Majors and Peter Breck (The Big Valley); David Carradine (Shane and Kung Fu); Ralph Taeger (Hondo); Neville Brand, William Smith and Philip Carey (Laredo); Christopher Jones (The Legend of Jesses James); Stuart Whitman (Cimarron Strip); Wayne Maunder (Custer); Leif Erickson, Cameron Mitchell and Henry Darrow (The High Chaparral); James Drury, Doug McClure and Lee J Cobb (The Virginian); Pete Duel and Ben Murphy (Alias Smith and Jones).

This is *my* list. Of the near-200 western television series made from the 1950s to the present day, these are the ones that made their mark – brand? – on me. Some readers will have their own favourites and lists and that's part of the joy of this fan thing.
More recent attempts to produce TV westerns have resulted in worthy, slow-moving yarns that try to apply modern political correctness to the wild frontier days. But, hope is always at hand whenever Tom Selleck and

Sam Eliott put on stetsons for television films. They seem to understand the genre perfectly and respect the traditionalist fans. Broadly, they take Louis L'Amour tales and the like and remain true to the beginning, middle and end school of storytelling.

Alternatively, the series Deadwood is an example of something that illustrated the rough, raw, dirty, profane nature of the Wild West but, whilst I enjoyed it, I don't love it. That may well have been the intention of the producers, to turn the wholesome notion of traditional western stories on it's ear, the way Leone and Peckinpah threw several changes into the mix on the big screen. Deadwood is to be admired, in my opinion, but not embraced by this kid.

The golden age of the TV western is over but through the wonders of DVD and the Internet, yesteryear is just a click away. In my head, it will never be over. Westerns will endure, to steal from Ethan Edwards in The Searchers, "as sure as the turning of the Earth".

IN FILMS

At the cinema, the major stars were, of course, John Wayne, James Stewart, Gary Cooper, Henry Fonda, Burt Lancaster, Robert Mitchum, Kirk Douglas, Randolph Scott, Joel McCrea, Audie Murphy, Glenn Ford, Robert Taylor, John Payne, Robert Ryan, Richard Widmark, Gregory Peck, Charlton Heston, Paul Newman, James Garner, Charles Bronson, James Coburn, Clint Eastwood and so many more. For reasons that escape me, I was never a big fan of Gene Autry or Hopalong Cassidy shows, enormously successful though they both were.

My favourite western film is The Searchers, starring John Wayne and directed by the masterful John Ford. I have watched it dozens of times and I can recite dialogue before the actors get a chance to open their mouths ("You speak pretty good American for a Comanche"). It is a thoughtful, emotional film, and an action-entertainment and character-rich story that shows what a great western can be.

But I enjoy lesser westerns too. The ones that were cranked out week by week in the 1940s and 1950s to satisfy the appetites of a ravenous viewing public still keep me entertained. These were the conveyor belt decades, before things moved on.

The 1960s gave us several classics – The Magnificent Seven, A Fistful of Dollars, The Good, The Bad And The Ugly, Once Upon A Time In The West, Butch Cassidy And The Sundance Kid, The Wild Bunch and True Grit, amongst others.

The 1970s delivered a real mixed bag including Bad Company, Billy Two Hats, Blazing Saddles, Buck And The Preacher, Chisum and Comes A Horseman.

The 1980s offered Heaven's Gate, The Long Riders, Silverado, Tom Horn, Pale Rider, Young Guns and more. But westerns as big box office draws were in decline.

The 1990s rallied a little with Wyatt Earp, Tombstone, Dances With Wolves, Maverick and Unforgiven, and the 2000s had Open Range, Hidalgo, Appaloosa, The Alamo and 3:10 To Yuma. More recently, the remake of True Grit was a big success and it sparked a healthy debate about who was the best Rooster. I know my choice – the hell I do.

Some of the westerns made after the 1960s show that in the right directorial hands, the genre can still boast amazing movies, but this is not meant to be a deep analysis of cowboy cinema, or else we'd be here all year.

However, I must not forget a nod to notable directors – John Ford, Raoul Walsh, Budd Boetticher, Michael Curtiz, Delmer Daves, Andre de Toth, Henry Hathaway, Henry King, Howard Hawks, Burt Kennedy, Anthony Mann, Andrew V McLaglen, Sam Peckinpah, John Sturges, Sergio Leone, King Vidor, William Wyler, Clint Eastwood, Kevin Costner and so many more.

To the writers, stunt teams, cinematographers, sound crews and all others behind the cameras, hats off to each and every one.

Apart from all the creative input, westerns on the big screen introduced me and many others to a significant stretch of American landscape known as Monument

Valley, part of the Colorado Plateau, on the Arizona-Utah state line. When I see John Wayne, James Stewart, Jack Elam and other stalwarts, my heart lifts, as I mentioned earlier. I would say the same for the sight of this extraordinary landscape. John Ford made films there and many more filmmakers have been seduced by the wonderful sandstone formations that western fans love to see. The director Peter Bogdanovich said:

"It's breathtaking. You can't believe it. It's very photogenic. It has a kind of mythic feeling of age, of legend. You've seen it in the movies, but when you see it in life, it's so epic in its proportions that it almost stands for the whole of the West."

My point, in this book of adoration, is to celebrate westerns and especially the character actors, bit-part players and journeymen performers that enriched many a reel. The supporting actors were the ingredients that made the difference and still make a difference to this man-child. When I see some of these actors and locations, I can get quite emotional but I disguise it by claiming that it's trail dust in my eyes, blowing in off the screen.

SUPPORTING ACTORS

Supporting actors were crucial to westerns on the big and small screens and over the years they became some of the most loved characters in celluloid history. I know this will make non-western fans' eyes glaze over but I just have to list these fine people (from memory, as they come to me):

Chill Wills, Harry Carey, Harry Carey Jr, John Carradine, Gabby Hayes, Ken Curtis, Hank Worden, Andy Devine, Slim Pickens, Rory Calhoun, Rod Cameron, Edgar Buchanan, Jay C Flippen, Robert J Wilke, L Q Jones, Iron Eyes Cody, Raymond Burr, Whit Bissell, John Larch, Hugh O'Brian, Arthur Hunnicut, Barton MacLane, Cesar Romero, Dub Taylor, Jim Davis, Dan Duryea, Frank Ferguson, Leo Gordon, Gene Evans, Royal Dano, R G Armstrong, Forrest Tucker, George Montgomery, Bruce Cabot, Strother Martin, Noah Beery, Noah Beery Jr, Ernest

Borgnine, Lee Van Cleef, Walter Brennan, Victor McLaglen, Ken Curtis, Jeff Chandler, Henry Brandon, Van Heflin, Arthur Kennedy, John Ireland, Jeff Corey, Ben Johnson, Dean Jagger, John McIntire, Ray Teal, Victory Jory, Paul Fix, Claude Akins, Rudolfo Acosta, Percy Helton, Ward Bond, Edmond O'Brien, Richard Jaeckel, Denver Pyle, Warren Oates, Dennis Hopper, Robert Duvall, Woody Strode, Sam Elliott, Bruce Dern, Jason Robards, Anthony Quinn, Lee Marvin, Jack Palance and George Kennedy.

Some of your favourite names may be missing and I fully acknowledge that some of these guys became bigger stars than others. But without them, whatever their star status, western films and TV shows would have been the poorer for their absence.

It will be noted that I have not mentioned any women in these meanderings and that is certainly not out of disrespect for the contributions made to the western genre by many fine actresses. It is just that on this nostalgic trip, this boy remembers the cowboys more than the cowgirls. That is not to say that there wasn't a frisson of adolescent excitement when Jane Russell appeared or the warm-hearted Katy Jurado or the bossy Barbara Stanwyck or the unsettling Marlene Dietrich or the deliciously waspish Maureen O'Hara. This is a politically incorrect boy's own trip! In this modern sensitive age of giving and taking offence too easily, I cannot nor do I have the inclination to defend this male stance. It was just the way it was when I was a nipper. Now let's get back to that list of supporting actors and the flaw within.

One person is missing (although I have dropped his name several times along the way, not least on the front cover of this effort) because I want him to be applauded all on his own as the greatest of them all, the one man who could play villains and buffoons, bad guys, good guys and those in between, the man with a face like no other, the actor that was impossible to ignore in films and on television from the mid-1940s to the mid-1990s.

Ladies and gentlemen,
join me as I salute and applaud……….

……………..Jack Elam.

The idea for the first part of this book is to create a tribute to this extraordinary actor who could play bad, bad guys in a good way and good, good guys in equally striking fashion. He could be mean, evil and menacing. He could be charming, benevolent and very funny.

I am twisting my own arm (metaphorically speaking, otherwise I would not be able to type) to name his best roles.

To catch Jack Elam at his nastiest, there is no finer example than the 1951 Tyrone Power and Susan Hayward movie Rawhide. He played Tevis, a psychopathic, gun-happy, ruthless, sneering outlaw. The chilling sequence where he threatens to shoot a toddler packs a powerful punch. He played mean to perfection. Then there is the opening sequence to Sergio Leone's Once Upon A Time In The West, with Elam as another mean character. It is memorable for the amazing sequence of him, in close-up, contorting and distorting his rubbery face to get rid of a fly. Elam has a relatively brief appearance at the beginning of the film because he soon gets gunned down by harmonica-playing Charles Bronson, but it encapsulates his movie persona beautifully as the villain's villain. It also uses his remarkable cartoonish facial features to magnificent effect. Unforgettable.

For comedy, we need look no further than Support Your Local Sheriff and Support Your Local Gunfighter, both with James Garner and both directed by Burt Kennedy. In Sheriff, Elam plays Jake and in Gunfighter, he's Jug May – and he has never been more entertaining or funny since his recurring Warner Brothers character Toothy Thompson in Tenderfoot and Bronco in the early 1960s.

The following pages feature some brief background information on Jack Elam and then come poems about him and in his honour, followed by a more general selection of western-themed pieces.

Saddle up and hear me out, pardners. I hope you enjoy the ride. Yes, Jack Elam (and others), I gave you the best years of my life – willingly.

JACK ELAM

JACK ELAM – BACKGROUND

Jack Elam was born William Scott Elam on 13 November somewhere between 1916 and 1920 (the exact year is disputed because Elam is said to have lied about his age to get work as a young man) in Miami, Gila County, Arizona, a former copper mining town. His father, Millard Elam, was an accountant. His mother, Amelia Kirby, died when Jack was around four years old. Young Jack lived with relatives after his mother's death but returned, aged about nine, to live with his father in California.

In a freak incident at a boy scout event, he lost the sight of an eye when another boy accidently stabbed him with a pencil. Initially, the loss of half his sight was a tragedy but as history would show, bizarrely, the remaining good eye *and* the bad one would become something of a beneficial trademark later in life.

Following in his father's footsteps, Jack studied accountancy and other business-related subjects and gained useful practice by helping his increasingly ailing

Dad with form-filling and other administrative chores. But as a partially-sighted young man, the strain of studying journals of figures and statistics became a burden and
Jack began to think of other ways to earn a living.
In his early working life, he spent time in the US Navy and managed a hotel but always found steady work back in business finances. While looking for an alternative career that was not dependent on two good eyes, luck played a part because some of his clients were Hollywood movie people and, occasionally, Elam traded his auditing and financial skills for small parts in pictures. One thing led to another and acting work began to emerge.

This was in the mid-1940s, the beginning of a golden age of western films, at first on the big screen and then, increasingly, on television. Most western features were simplistic good-versus-bad yarns, and Jack Elam, tall, skinny and not handsome by any stretch was ideal casting in villainous roles. He was to find out very quickly that losing the sight of an eye was going be advantageous rather than a drawback.

He was soon in demand for gangster films, thrillers and, of course, cowboy pictures. He was willing to take both credited and uncredited work as his new career progressed. A study of his movie CV tells us what we already know. His working life as an actor was dominated by westerns. For nearly thirty years, he was a bad guy mostly, until 1969 when he demonstrated a gift for comedy that no one had really noticed. His turn as Jake, alongside James Garner, in Support Your Local Sheriff is a joy to behold. His follow-up film with Garner, Support Your Local Gunfighter, with Elam as Jug, was equally superb.

In all, Jack Elam appeared in about 350 cinema features and television episodes. In 1983, he was awarded the Golden Boot in recognition of his contribution to westerns. In 1994, he was inducted into the Cowboy Hall of Fame.

He was married twice and was the father of two daughters and a son. He died on 20 October 2003. Western fans all over the world tipped their hats at the passing of this much-loved stalwart and oh-so familiar face.

The Guardian obituary said:

"With his bony, stubbled face, beetle-brows looming over a dead left eye, and gravelly voice, he was the very embodiment of a skulking, no-account, two-bit varmint, and the relish with which he played his parts made every appearance, however fleeting, a pleasure."

The New York Times said:

"His leer, bulging eye and precise acting skills transformed him from an accountant into one of the movies' most identifiable villains."

The Daily Telegraph said:

"He was always better-known as a face than as a name. Tall, weatherbeaten and effortlessly sinister, his grinning, wild appearance was enhanced by a wandering left eye. In Hollywood circles he was known as the good, the bad and the ugly."

The Radio Times said:

"His hangdog features, coupled with a dead left eye and wicked charisma, made him an unforgettable figure in westerns."

Clint Walker said:

"Well, I'll tell you, there was nobody like Jack but Jack. When you got to know him, he was a sweetheart."

Ty Hardin said:

"He could take a joke. He could go with the best and, believe me, the industry misses a man like this."

Jack Elam was, indeed, one of a kind.

JACK ELAM ON JACK ELAM

"I never presumed to be pretty."

"The toughest part of all, after you've worked out being an actor, is getting a job."

"In Rawhide, I was bad. I shot at a baby to make it dance, and I killed everybody in the picture except Tyrone Power and Susan Hayward. That's bad."

"It (his eye) does whatever the hell it wants."

"I was playing rotten, worthless guys in 95% of my pictures until that movie (Support Your Local Sheriff) came along. Since then (1969) I've played 95% comedy relief and plain, dull nice guys."

"The heavy today (late 1970s) is usually not my kind of guy. In the old days, Rory Calhoun was the hero because he was the hero and I was the heavy because I was the heavy, and nobody cared what my problem was. And I didn't either. I robbed the bank because I wanted the money. I've played all kinds of weirdos, but

I've never done the quiet, sick type. I never had a problem, other than the fact I was just bad."

"Who is Jack Elam?
Get me Jack Elam.
Get me a Jack Elam type.
Get me a young Jack Elam.
Who's Jack Elam"

Attributed to Jack Elam, as his definition of the career of a movie character actor

JACK ELAM 1

You were....

The Killer

Burvel Lambert

Henchman Raymond

Earl Boyce

Man at the bar

Arnie

Fargo

Henchman

Henchman number 2

Smiling Man

The Speaker

The Trader

Tevis

Cree

Eddie

Mort Geary

Mescal Jack

Gimp

Charlie

Dave Longden

Celestino Garcia

Harry Jackson

Pete Harris

Max Verne

Barton

Rusty Kolloway

Slim Strawboss

Castro

Vic

Whitey

Tim Lowerie

Matt Weber

Basra

Black Jack Ketchum

Newberry

Britt

Yost

Tex

Burger

Lee Dineen

Knife murderer

Shields

Charlie Max

Damen

Al

Reno Lawrence

Jack Miles

Chris Boldt

Hassan-Ben

Ivan

Father Matias

Ness Fowler

Shanks

McCoy

Pete

Slats Callahan

Tioga

Tom McLowery

Henry Bliss

Chris

Shotgun

Charlie Otis

Fatso Nagel

Gomez

Link Jerrod

Tony Molinor

Quint Avery

Luke Morgan

Arnold

Trooper Grimes

Wally Jobe

Flute

Clinton

Bill Ward

Perk Butler

Danny

Tim Renick

Phil Bricker

Dud Parsons

Luke Watson

Tug Swann

Jesse

Clell

Hock Ellis

Little Jimmy Lehigh

Cass

Dirk Ryan

Eli Roper

Clint Gannet

Toothy Thompson

Loper Johnson

Juan Cortina

Uncle Luce

Avery

Ed Hobbs

Horseface

Black Barr

Sim Groder

Gavin Martin

Gus Smith

Gates

Russell

Diamond

Dooley

Cheesecake

Joe Gage

Arnold Shaffner

Turkey Creek Jack Johnson

Flynn Hawks

Spence

Jake Wilson

Herm Forrest

Paul Henry

Stickface

Nick Bravo

Stan Wilinski

Jug Alverson

J D Smith

Calhoun Durango

Felix Gault

Charley Fox

Parson Hawks

Dobie

George Taggart

Petch

Deacon

Sam Urp

Deke Simons

Hank

Bellak

Preacher Weatherby

Ernest Scarnes

Sheriff Sam

Zack Slade

Diablo

Norman

Moon

Ace Williams

Slim Kovacs

Mackdin

Snaky

Blackner

Jake

Tom Mangrum

Sheriff Barnes

Harve Yost

Kittrick

John Wesley Hardin

Thompson

Phillips

Dodie Hoad

Buford Buckalaw

Honest John

Jug May

Kid Sheleen

Matt

Frank Clemens

Marcus Baxter

Boot Coby

Bitterroot

Pack Landers

Lucas Murdoch

Titus Spangler

Pierre

Grandad

Alamosa Bill

Marcus Taylor

Handy

Tuttle

Boss

Jarrod

King

Zack Wheeler

Joe Canton

Bad Jack Cutter

J Pete Hankins

Van Horn

Crazy Charlie

Cully Madigan

Trapper Willis

Jonas McBride

Willie Red Fire

Rattlesnake

Death Dreamer

Ira Bigelow

Big Mac

Avery Simpson

Frank

Sam Howard

Joe Simons

Seth Beaumont

Van Helsing

Captain O'Connell

Troscliar Boudreaux

Kid Corey

Hollis Buford

Clay Haller

Eli McQuade

Otto

Boot McGraw

Lum Witcher

Scrooge

Nick Turner

Dusty

Bud Krelman

Charlie

Squires

Tackett

Bully Stevenson

Jason Fitch

Esco Tokay

Boone

Skragg

Jake Calhoun

Hezekiah Crow

Dusty McHowell

Hick Peterson

Axel Ericson

Tommy

Grady

Buckshot

Curtis

…..you were all of these guys

in films, on TV,

but you were always

Jack Elam to me.

JACK ELAM 2

There was the tall, lean, lanky Jack,
All sneer and snide and toothy grin,
The one who gave the evil eye,
The one who could be bad as sin.

The one who cheated, the one who lied,
The one who laughed as victims died,
The one who robbed and double-crossed
The one who almost always lost.

There was the older, bulky, bearded Jack,
The rubber face, still that toothy grin,
The one who played it all for laughs
The one who took it on the chin.

Now Jack has gone, but he's never gone,
As long as there's a western on………

JACK ELAM 3

One eye looking at you,

One eye looking for you,

One eye trailing you around the room,

One eye eyeing you up to gun you down,

One eye giving you a quizzical look,

One eye summing you up,

One eye sending a shiver up your spine,

One eye bringing a smile to your lips,

One eye of the bandit,

One eye of the clown

One-eyed Jack,

One and only-eye Jack,

One and only Jack,

One Jack.

JACK ELAM 4

After Once Upon A Time In The West

Squeaking windmill wheel……

…..train station, God-forsaken place,
Man chalking on a wall, wide-eyed, beaky face,
Three men* appear, in long, duster coats,
Gunmen full of menace, grim as hell,
Whoever they are…..
…..ain't gonna end well.

Creaking floor, slamming doors,
Whistling wind, boots on boards,
Middle-of-nowhere random noise
Compensates for lack of words.

Strode deals with water drips,
Elam with a fly,
Mulock cracks his knuckles hard,
While they wait for another guy.

Train pulls in, package dropped,
Then off and on it's way,
No sight nor sound of the other guy,
So the three men walk away.

A harmonica wails in this nowhere place,
Just as they turn their backs,
A gentle sound floats on the wind,
And they look back to the tracks.

Three on one, truth to tell…..
…..it didn't end well…..

…..squeaking windmill wheel.

Woody Strode, Jack Elam, Al Mulock, and the "other" guy was Charles Bronson.

JACK ELAM 5

After Support Your Local Sheriff (Final Scene)

"Now the way this story ends is that they (James Garner's and Joan Hackett's characters) get married and he goes on to become Governor of the state. Never gets to Australia, but he keeps readin' a lot of books about it. I get to be sheriff of this town and then I go on to become one of the most beloved characters in Western folklore." Jake (Jack Elam)

He went on to become
One of the most beloved characters
In Western folklore,
As Jake, a kind of a joke,
But you know and I know
That a truer biographical word
Jack Elam never spoke.

MY FAVOURITE 10 JACK ELAM WESTERNS

1 Rawhide (1951)

- *Tyrone Power and Susan Hayward*

2 Support Your Local Sheriff (1969)

- *James Garner and Joan Hackett*

3 Rio Lobo (1970)

- *John Wayne*

4 Vera Cruz (1954)

- *Gary Cooper and Burt Lancaster*

5 Once Upon A Time In The West (1968)

- *Henry Fonda and Charles Bronson*

6 Support Your Local Gunfighter (1971)

- *James Garner and Suzanne Pleshette*

7 Hannie Caulder (1971)

- *Raquel Welch and Robert Culp*

8 The Over-The-Hill Gang (1969)

- *Walter Brennan and Edgar Buchanan*

9 The Man From Laramie
- *James Stewart and Arthur Kennedy*
10 Pat Garrett And Billy The Kid (1973)
- *James Coburn and Kris Kristofferson*

Some of these are great films and others less so, but Jack is great in all of them.

THE WEST, WESTERNS & ME

WHISKY WISDOM

"Talk low, talk slow and don't say too much." Anonymous

1

Don't approach a horse from the rear,

Don't approach a bull head on,

Don't approach a fool any which way,

And you and the world will get along.

2

If you don't achieve much in life,

Try - even if you fail because

It's better to be a contented has-been

Than a miserable never-was.

3.

Watch what you say and who you say it to,

If discretion is a quality you lack,

For if you let the cat out of the bag,

It's a hell of a lot harder to put it back

4.

Take some advice from an old cattleman,
I promise, I give you my word,
When thirsty in the midst of a cattle run,
Drink upstream from the herd.

5.

Sat in my rocking chair in the morning sun,
Sometimes a thought occurs,
So I offer you this sound advice,
Never squat while wearing your spurs.

6.

At the camp fire supper, study your plate,
And be sure what you can see,
Not what it is in the gravy pool
But what it used to be.

7.

Sometimes you meet some strange ones,
Like the uneducated son of a dope
Who's not sure if he's just lost his horse
Or found a new piece of rope.

8.

Call me lucky, call me cute,
Call me a fortunate soul,
Call me winner of the poker pot,
Call me butter 'cos I'm on a roll.

9.

To strike a balance in this life of choices,
Of risks and chances and tempting voices,
Always keep a rein on your yearnings
And don't let them outstrip your earnings.

10.

When you start getting short answers like nope and yup,
You know that's the time for you to shut up.

OPEN RANGE

"It's a shame to go forever without takin' a taste of somethin'."
Boss Spearman, Open Range

Our small front garden

Was a huge prairie -

Over there, an ambush in the gulch,

And there, an attack in the canyon,

Down there, we cut them off at the pass,

Our saloon was on the edge of the rockery,

Our O.K. corral, our fort, our Dodge City,

Wherever we wanted them to be,

Our ranch as sprawling as our minds,

No fences to restrict

The open range of our imagination.

WEE TOMATO BAG

"There's a little cowboy in all of us, a little frontier." Louis L'Amour

My mother,
Forever wise in the ways of the world,
Knowledgeable, sensible,
Always to be trusted,
Would tell this young son
That when a cowboy was wounded,
It wasn't real blood,
It was just that his "wee tomato bag"
Got busted.

KID CUSHNAN

"Boots, chaps and cowboy hats – nothing else matters."
Anonymous

The arm of the chair was more than an arm,
It was my horse as a kid while watching TV,
I watched all the westerns and lived every second,
For there on the screen I swore it was me.

I was James Garner, I was Bret Maverick,
I was Will Hutchins, I was Tom Brewster,
I was Clint Walker, I was Cheyenne Bodie,
I was Ty Hardin, I was Bronco Layne,
I was Robert Fuller, I was Jess Harper,
I was Michael Landon, I was Joe Cartwright,
I was Fess Parker, I was Davy Crockett,
I was James Arness, I was Matt Dillon,
I was Richard Boone, I was Paladin,
I was Clayton Moore, I was the Lone Ranger,
I was Jock Mahoney, I was the Range Rider,
I was Clint Eastwood, I was Rowdy Yates,

I was Dale Robertson, I was Jim Hardie,
I was Steve McQueen, I was Josh Randall,
I was Robert Horton, I was Flint McCullough,
I was Doug McClure, I was Trampas,
I was Cameron Mitchell, I was Buck Cannon,
I was Pete Duel, I was Hannibal Heyes.

I can't imagine my life without western heroes,
The stetsons they wore and how they were dressed,
I felt the excitement of theme songs and music,
Saddling up on the chair and riding out west.

LITTLE JOE

"Life is too short. Ride your best horse first." Anonymous

It is no longer there
But I can see the gnarled tree stump
That used to be a horse
In a wild, wild western game,
Occupying a corner
Of St Teresa's school playground.
At my turn, I was often
Little Joe of Bonanza fame.

The mixing of the childish
And the creative
Produced something
Of what I am today.
The uneven, rough
Knobbly, insect-ridden bark
Left ragged skin marks,
And in my head, clear,
Smooth memories of important
Childhood and cowboy stuff.

GUNSHOT

"You always fancied yourself faster than me. Draw, you tinhorn."
Steve Judd, Ride The High Country

When I played Cowboys and Indians as a kid,
My gunshot noise was a kind of throat-clearing rasp,
Before waiting a second to hear my friend
Play-act at dying with a grunt and a gasp.

Our first guns were our hands,
Fists clenched, forefingers extended,
Fun for hours, rough and tumble,
No harm as long as we pretended.

The first time I heard real gunshots
Outside our house in those "Troubles" years,
I let out a throat-clearing rasp, a dry-cry,
No fun, just the sound of the sum of my fears.

BURNING MAP

"Truth is something that always comes back at you, isn't it?" Ben Cartwright, Bonanza

I remember the places,

Reno,

Carson City,

Virginia City,

And a mass of land,

The Ponderosa,

The big yellow word "Bonanza"

Zooming up from nowhere

And from the dot that was Virginia City

Flames destroying the map,

Four riders revealed,

The Cartwrights.

The fifth rider,

No one could see,

Way out west, in West Belfast,

Was me.

GUNFIGHTER BALLADS & TRAIL SONGS

After the 1959 Marty Robbins LP

I watched the movies,
I watched TV,
I read the books
Played this LP.

I posed in the mirror
Lost in the grooves,
Mimed all the songs
With cowboy moves.

Side One:
Big Iron
Cool Water
Billy The Kid
A Hundred And Sixty Acres
They're Hanging Me Tonight
The Strawberry Roan

Side Two:
El Paso
In The Valley
The Master's Call
Running Gun
The Little Green Valley
Utah Carol

For this daydreaming cowboy,
35 minutes and 25 seconds
of wonder, adventure, romance,
excitement and joy.

GUNSLINGER

"If you're gonna use that gun, you better start on me." Marshall Matt Dillon, Gunsmoke

The gunslinger lies

Bleeding to death,

Resisting his last breath.

A crowd gathers.

They know his name.

They see his shame.

Once the fastest

Draw in the west,

Now lying second best.

MOMENTS

"I won't be wronged. I won't be insulted. I won't be laid a hand on. I don't do these things to other people, and I require the same from them." John Bernard Books, The Shootist

Moments.

Moments of silence.

Moments of pure silence.

Then the scrape

Of a gun from leather,

A bang echoing out towards the mountains,

A bullet finding it's target.

A body.

A body lying still.

A body lying still in the dust.

Moments.

Moments of silence.

Moments of pure silence.

Then the gathering, shuffling,

Murmuring crowd.

COWBOY DRIFTER

"A man has to be what he is, Joey. Can't break the mould. I tried it and it didn't work for me." Shane

Ride the dusty haze
From here to sunset
Past ramshackle towns.

Smell the buffalo,
Feel your dry throat,
The pain of riding,
The weight of the gun,
The pure loneliness,

The oneness of one.

SHOTGUN

"If there's anything I don't like, it's driving a stagecoach through Apache country." Buck, Stagecoach

I'm riding shotgun on a stagecoach,
Hat brim flat against my head,
Rifle nestling in my arms,
Wishing it was you instead.

Across the plains from here to there,
Desert wind blinds dusty eyes,
Bumps and bruises from the trail,
That's the job, it's no surprise.

I dream of rocking chairs and sunsets,
I'm just a poor old son of a gun,
I need you now, we need our time,
My working days are almost done.

The danger's high, the pay is low,
The land both beautiful and bleak,

I've been attacked, I've shot and killed,
I am as strong as I am weak.

Sunrise, sundown, shadows, shapes,
Trigger ready, eyes sharp and wide,
One more trail for my aching bones
And these shotgun days will subside.

But what is that out in the distance,
Fifty, a hundred, it's hard to tell,
Me and the driver exchanging glances,
One more trail, the trail to hell.

I'm riding shotgun on a stagecoach,
In this God-forsaken place,
Rifle cocked and more than ready,
Inside my head, I see your face.

BOUNTY HUNTER

"When the law put up the money, the bounty hunter put on his guns." Poster slogan for The Bounty Hunter

He began as a dot
Some way away
And slowly, slowly, slowly
Through the shimmering heat
He became more of an ink blot,
Then more of a paint splash,
An abstract shape on the move,
Closer and closer and closer,
Bigger and bigger and bigger,
Human-shaped, man-shaped,
An imposing figure,
Armed and ready,
Chasing us, catching us
And then doing God-knows-what to us.

GUN OR FIST

"Somebody oughta belt you in the mouth....." George Washington McLintock, McLintock

The passion for revenge

Outweighs

The compassion of forgiveness,

The eye for an eye,

The urge to punish,

To condemn, to get even,

To gain an upper hand

Above and beyond reason

And the desire to understand.

The naturalness of violence,

Impossible to resist

In the wildness of this wilderness,

A choice of gun or fist.

WILD WEST

"We deal in lead, friend." Vin, The Magnificent Seven

Unshaven men, cheroots in their mouths,
So many norths, so many souths,
Different directions, wide open lives,
No time for children, no time for wives.
Each town is the same as the others they've been,
Same stores and saloons, all things in between,
Lonesome and lost and best left alone,
Unfriendly faces carved out of stone.

Into saloons through two swinging doors,
Looking around at the drunks and the whores,
Pick out the victims and call them to draw,
No room for emotions, no place for the law.
Gunslingers looking for something to do,
Always for hire regardless of who,
Someone must love them each mother's son,
But their closest companions are a horse and a gun.

VENGEANCE

"Are you gonna pull those pistols or whistle Dixie?" Josey Wales, The Outlaw Josey Wales

Vengeance is the way of the untamed,
The unwritten code of the wronged and the pissed,
In this age of the righteous and the unforgiven,
The only way to exist.

In the blue-black haze, I see an outline
And I reach out to touch nothing
As shapes and shadows play tricks
With my eyes.

There is nothing there, never has been,
But soon will come the day,
The day of reckoning, the day of the avenger,
The day of surprise.

Soon will come the day.

WITNESS

"I seldom forget a face or a sum of money." Paladin, Have Gun Will Travel

I saw it,

I witnessed it,

I confirm it.

You didn't see it,

You didn't witness it,

You can't confirm it.

It's my word against your word.

You can't rely on me.

I can't rely on you.

The truth is out there,

So am I, so are you.

So is..

HUNTED

"I've killed just about everything that walks or crawled at one time or another." Will Munny, Unforgiven

Behind me,
The crack of a snapping twig.

Look around, scan the trees
And the gaps in between,
Listen beyond the breeze,
Nothing more heard, nothing seen.

Who or what?
A dog, a wolf,
A scavenger, a crazy man,
A bandit, a ghost,
Fairies, elves?

Twigs don't snap themselves.

AFTER THE MASSACRE

"Nothing in this world is more surprising than the attack without mercy!" General Custer, Little Big Man

There was nothing left for the sun to burn,
Nothing for fire to destroy,
Nothing left but ashes and soil
And what was there can never return.

There was no more breath, no more life,
No signs of anything moving around,
Except the dust in ghostly swirls
And breezy wails the only sound.

There was nothing left to identify,
No epitaph to carve in stone,
Who worked this land and what they did
Will never, ever, ever be known.

The lone rider inhaled, his breath a hiss,
Then whispered to his very soul:
"It don't get more lonely than this."

SERMON

"Nothing like a good piece of hickory." Preacher, Pale Rider

Eye for eye,

Tooth for tooth,

Lie for lie,

Truth for truth,

Easy to loathe, to despise,

Harder to forgive and compromise,

Easier to attack, to shoot to kill,

Than find the way, than find the will,

To navigate the road to peace,

To find the patience, to do it well,

To climb to heaven

Or slide to hell.

We have a voice,

We have a choice..........

RATTLESNAKE

'Don't interfere with somethin' that ain't botherin' you none."
Anonymous

A yell at the Eagle Ranch, Arizona:
"Rattlesnake!"
We stopped, turned about face,
Our chores on hold as the foreman ran
To the steps of the outhouse, hiding place
Of this unexpected but always expected guest.

This big guy with a long stick and deep container
Gently created some dust, no fuss, no commotion,
Until the snake emerged to be lifted by the stick-end
And dropped into the bucket in one smooth motion,
Applauded by us gaping, in awe, impressed.

The snake, released a hundred yards away,
Slithered and slid and was soon gone
And we were even more respectful
Of the ground we walked upon.

GHOST TOWN

'When you hear a strange sound, drop to the ground." Harmonica, Once Upon A Time In The West

I had come to the edge of town
Because I had to see what I refused to believe,
Where once the streets were full of life,
There was nothing, nothing at all,
Just boarded stores and a dusty wind,
No people, no traffic, no litter, nothing,
Where once local pride was a proud boast,
Now Boom Town had become a ghost.

PIONEERS

"I get paid to worry and I intend to earn my keep." Major Seth Adams, Wagon Train

Beyond that tree,
Beyond the next,
Beyond that one,
Is the land of dreams,

No distance, not much,
Almost close enough to touch.

We have to plan a route,
Navigate obstacles and traps,
Assess risks,
For it is not as easy as it seems,

So near, yet so far,
For who we were, who we are,
To reach over there, to see
Who we will be.

LAST STOP

"I'm halfway to hell and looking for help." Cable Hogue, The Ballad of Cable Hogue

I'm sitting in Brentwood station,
The night is cold around me,
The thought of your last kiss
Makes me sigh.

I'm watching the night sky,
A curtain of falling rain
Cannot hide the moon
Or my urge to cry.

Miles away from home,
Never felt so low,
No one seems to care,
No one wants to know.

You're dancing in my mind,
My thoughts are playing a game,

I hear your voice in the darkness,
So far, yet so near.

The train pulls into the station,
I feel a tug, an order to stand,
I'm handcuffed to a Marshall,
The time is here.

Miles away from you,
No chance to say goodbye,
Tomorrow a court will judge
This man will have to die.

RELENTLESS

"He didn't deserve a chance. If he wanted a chance, he should have gone somewhere else." Judge Roy Bean, The Life and Times of Judge Roy Bean

Chasing,

Chasing,

Chasing,

A man on the run,

Riding,

Riding,

Riding,

To the horizon,

To the end of the Earth,

And on through the eye of the sun.

SEARCHING

"That'll be the day." Ethan Edwards, The Searchers

In the doorway,

A choice to settle

Or succumb to answer

The horizon's call.

In the doorway,

Inside, a family,

Outside, the familiar

And the gamble of the unknown,

To stay

Or ride away.

THE MAN CALLED DUKE

John Wayne 1907 – 1979

From the Ringo Kid in Stagecoach
To The Shootist's J B Books,
No one could out-cowboy
The man they called The Duke.
From Fort Apache to Red River,
Yellow Ribbon and Rio Grande,
No one could walk and talk
Like this far from quiet man.

Ethan Edwards in The Searchers,
John T Chance in Rio Bravo,
Tom Doniphon in Liberty Valance,
Cole Thornton in El Dorado.
He made so much more than westerns,
But he was the perfect fit,
Saluted in his later years
For Rooster in True Grit.

THE MAN CALLED PAPPY

John Ford 1894 – 1973
"My name is John Ford and I make westerns."
John Wayne called Director John Ford "Pappy"

Stagecoach

Drums Along The Mohawk

My Darling Clementine

Fort Apache

3 Godfathers

She Wore A Yellow Ribbon

Wagon Master

Rio Grande

The Searchers

The Horse Soldiers

Sergeant Rutledge

Two Rode Together

The Man Who Shot Liberty Valance

How The West Was Won (segment)

Cheyenne Autumn

Might be a list to you, but it's poetry to me!

THE MAN CALLED PECKINPAH

Sam Peckinpah 1925 – 1984

The Deadly Companions
Ride The High Country
Major Dundee
The Wild Bunch
The Ballad of Cable Hogue
Junior Bonner
Pat Garrett & Billy The Kid

Yes, there was blood,
Yes, there was gore,
But there was so much more.

THE MAN CALLED MANN & THE MAN CALLED JIMMY

Anthony Mann 1906 – 1967
James Stewart 1908 - 1997

Bend Of The River

The Naked Spur

The Far Country

The Man From Laramie

Winchester '73

Starring James, aw, aw, Stewart,

Aw, TV Sunday matinees

In my, aw, aw, days as a kid,

My, aw, aw, golden age,

My, aw, aw, glory days.

THE MAN CALLED COOP

Gary Cooper 1901 – 1961

"If you asked me
If I'm the luckiest guy in the world,
All I can say is yup," he said,
But it wasn't entirely true,
For we were the lucky ones
To watch and enjoy
His westerns
And all he would say and do.

One of the very best,
Big, slow and easy,
Man of the west.

THE RIFLE CALLED WINCHESTER

Born 1873

History tries to tell us
How the West was won,
All across the prairies
And under the desert sun.

Some exaggeration,
Sometimes lack of tact,
Sometimes flights of fancy
Sometimes honest fact.

But one thing is for certain,
No one can dare contest,
The Winchester repeating rifle
Was the gun that won the West.

LAST ROUND-UP

In my DVD collection, I have a TV special called When The West Was Fun: A Western Reunion, made in 1979 and presented by Glenn Ford. The show takes place in a saloon and features many of my television western heroes.

It is a celebration of the westerns I've mentioned in this book and it is lovely to watch, if a little scrappy and cack-handed in it's set pieces and conversations.

A significant number of actors from the glory days walk through the swinging doors at the beginning and the DVD is awash with little clips of many of the series I watched as a kid.

If I want to be reminded of a happy childhood, I know that one of the things I can do is stick this disc into the player and drift back to some very contented times.

I have included a number of lists in this book, much to the chagrin of some readers, no doubt, but hopefully the fans of cowboy movies and TV shows will have gotten a kick out of remembering and being reminded of this trove of screen treasure.

Compiling a book like this has become easier, thanks to technology, especially the Internet and the many research sites that have gathered information, all kinds of clips, full TV episodes and complete feature films. A substantial amount of the material in this effort has come from my own head, a sign of brilliant recall or an illustration of madness. But help has been in the ether whenever I hit a mental block.

I wanted to find something appropriate to end the book and I discovered a recording of an awards ceremony that I think will help me round things off.

Jane Russell (frisson) and Jack Elam were the presenters at the 1996 National Cowboy Hall of Fame event that was honouring Audie Murphy and Ernest Borgnine. There is a lovely moment when Borgnine, after embracing Miss Russell, hugs Elam and gives him a kiss on the cheek.

"Jack said, if you kiss me, I'll kill you," he beamed. Then he went on to say:

"Well, it's been a long road. If I get a little choked up, don't mind me. My heart's on my sleeve tonight. You know, I'm recalling when I was a kid playing Cowboys and Indians. We used to get our nickel every week, a penny if you could afford it to buy some candy, and we'd go to the movies and watch these great heroes – Buck Jones, Tom Mix, Hoot Gibson, oh Lordy, just great people. We never met them but we believed every word they said. And then we went out and played these cowboys.

Little in my wildest imagination did I ever think I would be playing later in motion pictures. It's just incredible. I guess I have had an incredible life. I never dreamed I would ever be an actor and yet I became one, simply because my mother said: "You always like to make a damn fool of yourself in front of people, why don't you give it a try? And it hit my chord and I said Mom "I'll do it."

I was very lucky. Ten years later, I had an Academy Award, believe it or not, and I was so grateful. And I am so grateful this evening to be included in the

*company of Audie Murphy. What a privilege. Really.
I gave Jack Elam his little horse up here two years ago
and inadvertently I said: "I made westerns too."
Nobody paid any attention.....but, boy, am I happy
tonight.
My wife was over there squeezing my hand just now
and it's just the greatest thrill in the world to be
included and to think that I am part of this great Hall of
Fame - the names, the people, the honour. I shall not
forget this ever. To me, this is another Academy Award
and I thank you ever so much.
Thank you Jack. And I'd like to thank my dear friends
who came, like a gentleman called Burt Kennedy, one
of the finest and greatest western directors I've ever
seen in my life. We had a time."*

Throughout his speech, Ernest Borgnine was very emotional but he managed to convey something of the enduring appeal of westerns, the love they stirred up in kids who liked action and adventure in a certain setting. I related to his thoughts, as I hope I have illustrated in these pages. I was also thrilled to see the affection between Borgnine and this book's mascot, Mr Jack Elam.

Thank you, Jack. We never met.

But we had a time!

So, there it is. My trip down memory lane. My attempt to celebrate westerns.

I hope you enjoyed it.

I am a freelance writer and I can be contacted for writing commissions and other media contributions at joecushnan@aol.com

I am always pleased to hear from readers.

Happy trails!

Books by Joe Cushnan, widely available in paperback on most online bookselling sites and some available in Kindle format ;

Business:
Retail Confidential
Much Calamity & The Redundance Kid
Rolling In The Aisles
Customer Service In A Nutshell

Poetry:
Geek! Poems Because Of The Music
A Belfast Kid
Hamish Sheaney: The Nearly-Man Of Irish Literature
Only Yules & Verses
Only Drools & Corsets
The Chuckle Files
Juggling Jelly
A Bumper Bundle Of Funny Poems

Film Biography:
Stephen Boyd: From Belfast To Hollywood

Crime Fiction:
Belfast Backlash – A Sticky Miller & Limp Donnelly Crime Story